The Perfect Cake
for a Lady

Karen Bernardo

Storybites Press
Vestal, NY 13850
www.storybites.com

ISBN: 978-0-9985744-3-1

DEDICATION

To my husband David, whose unwavering support enables me to follow my dreams; to my daughter Julie, whose passion for decorating cupcakes fueled my imagination; and to my granddaughter Sarah, who inspired "the cake story" in the first place.

Chapter One
Monday, February 2
3:20 p.m.

On the second floor of a tiny apartment in Binghamton, New York, Rose Bevelacqua was packing up Christmas decorations and unpacking Valentine hearts. When she moved from her spacious three-bedroom house in Endicott into this one-bedroom subsidized flat, she'd had to get rid of almost everything that made a house a home. The mahogany dining room table that had seen so many happy holiday dinners; the Italian provincial bedroom suite with its double dressers and queen-sized bed; the white wicker patio set with the big puffy cushions—all were gone. But she'd made sure to save her holiday decorations. Even if Rose didn't have a big house to decorate and little children to delight, the decorations made her happy every time she changed them, and happiness was important.

She extracted a handcrafted calico wreath from the middle of the Rubbermaid tote and carried it out to the front door. By "front door" she meant, of course, the door that separated her apartment from the hallway and the incursion of the outside world. In moving to Madison Manor, she'd hoped to find some compatible friends like the ones she had on the North Side of Endicott—Italian-American widows with whom she could can tomatoes and knit baby hats and exchange recipes.

But in the two years she'd been there, that hadn't happened. When she first moved in, her next door neighbor kept accusing Rose of stealing her mail. Down the hall had lived a man who could tell you the *New York Times* headline for any day in the past fifty years, but couldn't tell you much else. Both of them had moved, thank God. But in the fall, their apartments had been leased to a nosy old Jewish man and a needy girl with some sort of mental diagnosis. On the first floor lived the Changs who only spoke Chinese, the Espositos who only spoke Spanish, and the Khans and the Tinkasinghs who spoke God knew what. Rose sat with the Espositos at Mass sometimes, but they weren't great conversationalists.

Rose sighed, remembering her church in Endicott, St. Theresa's. All her Endicott widows still went there, but Rose couldn't get a bus on Sunday mornings early enough to make St. Theresa's 9 o'clock Mass. (She hadn't realized the bus issue when she agreed to move into Madison Manor, because that might have been a deal-breaker.) On the other hand, at St. Casimir's in Binghamton she'd come to know Father Zelinsky, whom she adored, and she'd fallen in with a small but vibrant community of mostly Polish widows who liked to cook as much as she did. But they didn't live in her building, or even on her street, so it wasn't the same.

The nail on which the Christmas wreath hung sagged limply in the lauan door and fell out entirely when Rose removed the wreath. Recalling the sturdy oak door in her house in Endicott, Rose sighed and retreated back into her apartment for a hammer and a larger nail. A few quick raps secured the new nail into the door, but also attracted the attention of her elderly neighbor, who—attired in brown suspenders, a green plaid shirt and a yellow bow tie—came into the hall to see what was going on.

"You should get some of those Command hooks," he observed, padding toward her in stocking feet. "No pounding needed. Stick to the wall. They're made by 3M, the Scotch tape people."

6

"Probably so, Mr. Zimmerman," Rose said. "Right now I just want to get my decorations up."

"Murray," he suggested. "I've told you to call me Murray. Mr. Zimmerman's my father. Are you having a party?"

Rose gave him a sideward glance, finding it incredible that anyone as ancient as Murray Zimmerman had ever had a father. "No. When I had a house and the kids were little, I used to decorate for every holiday. And I still do."

Murray nodded sagely. "Tradition. It's important when you get to be our age."

Rose sniffed; Murray looked to be at least eighty-five, and she'd only turned seventy-four the previous June.

She backed up and looked at her wreath critically. "I think that's good, don't you?"

"No," Murray said. "I think it's upside down."

"It's patchwork. How can it be upside down?"

Murray pointed a gnarled finger toward the bottom section. "All the hearts on that patch are pointing up."

"Well, the ones on the patch next to it are pointing left," Rose said. "They're supposed to be random."

"Hmm." Murray got so close to the wreath his nose nearly touched it. "Not sure I like that. The universe was created with order and method. And why are those ballerinas waving flags?"

"They're not ballerinas. They're winterguard performers." She sighed in exasperation. "It's sort of a combination of twirling and dance—my granddaughter Parker is in a winterguard troupe, and they sold these wreaths as a fundraiser."

He shook his head. "Doesn't make it any better. Do you have a different wreath?"

"Not for Valentine's Day." The more Rose stared at the offending wreath, the less she liked it herself.

Murray hadn't taken his eyes off it either. "Maybe if you wrapped some ribbon around it, it would break up the pattern. Or distract the eye from the ballerinas. You know what you should do? You should ask Betsy. The bakery closes at three, so she should be here any time. And it will mean a lot to her that you asked her advice."

"Why would I ask Betsy's advice? She wears clothes she finds in the dumpster!" Rose snatched the wreath off the door and went back inside. She was certainly not going to ask decorating advice from a nutjob like Betsy Mangero.

Pudgy, pockmarked Betsy had been placed at Madison Manor by some social service agency that helped her get a job at a bakery downtown, where she was apparently in some kind of training program. But Betsy's background stuck to her like a bad smell. She desperately needed a mother, and with no encouragement from Rose, she had apparently decided that Rose fit the bill.

Every day when she came home, Betsy announced her arrival by clomping up the stairs and hollering "Mrs. B! Mrs. B!" If Rose opened the door (sometimes she didn't), Betsy would regale her with the most interesting tidbits of her day, and display her most novel acquisitions. The plastic Hello Kitty purse she'd found in a dumpster behind the old Metrocenter. The kitchen chair that needed "just a little dot of glue" to make it semi-stable. The wrapped sub she found lying on a park bench – "and it was still warm!" Betsy saw nothing wrong, to say nothing of unpalatable, with finishing other people's lunches and absconding with other people's discards. And there was often a long and convoluted story surrounding the item's discovery that Rose just didn't want to hear.

Although Rose was admittedly lonely, she wanted as little to do with her neighbors as possible. She could hear her mother's voice: *this is what happens when all sorts of people mix together. People should stay with their own kind.* Her mother had not wanted to leave Italy, just as Rose had not wanted to leave the north side of Endicott. But after Rose used most of the money Dom left her to pay their son Anthony's medical and funeral expenses, she just couldn't afford to keep the house. The social worker had suggested Madison Manor; it was on the bus line Rose needed even if it didn't have an early Sunday morning run, and the subsidy had made the rent manageable.

She knelt down next to the Rubbermaid tote of decorations and opened a good-sized shoebox labeled "Valentine." On top lay a little napkin holder made of two wooden hearts glued to a flat base. "Best Mom Ever— Vincent" was scrawled across the pink heart in a shaky script. Rose smiled and set that on the floor; Vincent, now a cop, had done well for himself, but his handwriting hadn't improved much.

Next out of the box came china salt-and-pepper shakers—the salt shaker a light pink and the pepper a dark rose. She set those next to the napkin holder, and held up Vincent and Anthony's pink and red suncatchers to glow in the late afternoon sun; they would look lovely in her kitchen window. The tiny gold windchime of entwined hearts that Dom bought at Boldt Castle would go right alongside.

Digging deeper into the box, Rose unwrapped a bundle of tissue to reveal her granddaughter Parker's contribution —a kitten made from half a walnut, glued to a pink felt base. Then she started to unfold a table runner her daughter Diane, Parker's mother, had bought at a craft show at Binghamton University. As she did so, several tiny brown pellets bounced across the floor. Mouse droppings, and sure enough, there was an uneven hole gnawed in the runner's lace trim. Rose spun the shoebox around and found the telltale hole where the mouse had gained entry.

She rocked back on her heels in dismay. It served her right for leaving the lid off the tote because she didn't want to squash the delicate pysanki quail eggs on the Easter wreath. Everything in this whole tote would need to be washed—and some of the things, like Vincent's napkin holder, couldn't be.

Cursing her bad knees, she used a kitchen chair to haul herself to her feet. She'd hoped that rubbing the items lightly with some disinfectant sprayed on a soft towel might do the trick—but while this did no damage to the suncatchers or the shakers, even the gentlest of touches took some of the red poster paint off the base of the napkin holder. Rose sank back onto the floor and tears welled in her eyes. All she'd wanted to do was decorate her new home the way she always had her old one, and preserve these delicate mementos of her old life. Was that too much to ask?

Suddenly, however, something new piqued her ears. It was Betsy, definitely—but she wasn't clomping up the stairs, she was racing up them—and she wasn't calling out to see if Rose was home, she was shrieking as if her life depended on it.

Chapter Two
Monday, February 2
3:30 p.m.

"Mrs. B! Mrs. B!"

Rose didn't exactly leap to her feet. But she did manage to work herself into a position her daughter's yoga instructor called "downward facing dog" and struggle upwards from there. In the process she murmured a brief prayer to St. Jude, patron saint of lost causes. Betsy was a lost cause if ever there was one, and Rose didn't know if she was praying for the girl or for herself.

Rose opened her door just as Betsy appeared at the top of the steps, red-faced and panting. "Mrs. B, he's going to kill me!"

"Nobody's going to kill you," Rose said firmly.

"He is! He knows where I live!"

"Well, I know where you live, and *I'm* going to kill you if you don't stop yelling like that."

Murray Zimmerman unexpectedly emerged from the apartment next to Betsy's. "I heard screaming," he said.

"So did I," Rose said as she hustled Betsy into her living room, slammed the door in Murray's face, and pushed the still-wailing Betsy into an overstuffed chair. "Seriously, you keep up that racket, and I'll get the police to take you away!"

Being "taken away" by a cop was the worst possible threat in Betsy's view, and Rose knew it. Betsy took a deep gulping breath.

"A serial killer—came into—the bakery," she gasped at last.

"Oh, please," Rose said. "A serial killer? What did he look like?"

"Grey suit—grey hair—grey hat—silver eyes."

"You mean hazel eyes," Rose corrected.

Betsy shook her head vigorously. "Silver. Metal."

"Nobody has metal eyes."

"This guy did."

Rose sighed. "I can't believe I'm saying this, but I want the whole story."

"I was all alone in the bakery—"

"What happened to the rest of the staff?"

"Justin Hopko had finished the baking and left for school. Eileen Reeves—she decorates the cakes—called in sick. And Samantha Truesdell—she's the owner—was at some Chamber thing. But I want to tell you about the serial killer."

"Please do," said Rose.

"He showed up at the bakery at about one-thirty, walking back and forth in front of the glass doors and looking in."

"And you saw his metal eyes."

"No," Betsy said. "He was too far away for me to see his eyes right then. He kept looking in the shop and then glancing back and forth up and down the street, like he was worried someone would see him."

"So what did you do?"

"I was on the phone talking to Carl—"

"Is Carl your boyfriend?" Rose seriously couldn't imagine Betsy having a boyfriend.

"Oh, no," Betsy said. "I like Greg. Carl's his roommate."

"They're college students?"

"Grad students at Binghamton University. Greg is majoring in music performance—"

Rose couldn't care less what Greg was majoring in, to say nothing of Carl. "So you were talking to Carl, and I presume you hung up to wait on your customer."

"I did. And I put the phone on the counter, not in my cleavage."

"Excuse me?"

"Samantha says it's tacky to put your phone in your cleavage, but where else are you going to put it? My work pants don't have pockets."

She had a point, Rose thought. "Then the man must have come inside, because you saw his eyes."

Betsy nodded. "It gives me the creeps just to think of it."

"What did he say?"

"This is really weird, Mrs. B. He asked me to recommend the perfect cake for a lady."

"That's a dumb thing to say," Rose said. "All ladies don't like the same kind of cake."

"That's what I told him—not the dumb part," Betsy said. "I was more polite than that—I told him every lady is different. So he asked me what kind of cake I liked best, and I said Black Forest."

"What's Black Forest?"

"It's a dark chocolate cake with a cherry filling. Then there's whipped cream on top with little chocolate shavings all over it. There was one in the plexiglas case on the counter. I pointed to it and told him it was my favorite cake."

"Did he buy it?"

"Yeah. I just wanted him to pay me and get out. He made me really nervous."

"Why?"

"It was his metal eyes, and the way he touched my phone."

"Your phone?" Rose asked. "What was he doing with your phone?"

"He kept stroking it, waking it up, and I don't like that but I was afraid to take it away from him. I couldn't wait for him to leave, and when he did, I was so relieved. But then, when I got home, I saw his cake on the front steps."

Rose did a double take. "Whose steps?"

"Our steps. Right downstairs. There's a slice of Black Forest cake on our front steps."

Rose flew to the window. One floor below, Murray Zimmerman sat in the sunshine on the concrete steps, feeding chocolate crumbs to a squirrel from a china plate. Beside the plate, a long silver knife glinted in the sun.

She spun back to face Betsy. "How did it get there? I mean, how did the guy know where you live?"

"That's my point, Mrs. B!" Betsy's pockmarked, mottled face became even more flushed. "He came to the bakery a little after lunchtime! He couldn't possibly have followed me home, since the cake was already on the steps when I got here!"

Rose's first thought was "stalker," but who would stalk Betsy? She wasn't pretty, she wasn't rich, she wasn't famous. Someone would have to be a lunatic to stalk Betsy, and the idea of a lunatic right outside her building demanded action.

She whirled around again and flung the window open. "Murray Zimmerman! Stop feeding that squirrel!"

The squirrel darted away, and Murray looked up, baffled. "What's the matter with you? Do you have a thing against squirrels?"

"Just bring the plate upstairs—no, wait! On second thought, don't touch it!" Rose dashed over to the cordless phone on the end table. "It might be evidence! I'm going to call Vincent!"

14

Chapter Three
Monday, February 2
3:40 p.m.

"You called me to Madison Manor to look at a plate?" Vincent demanded, standing on the front steps.

At his side, a docile policewoman slipped the china plate, crumbs and all, into an evidence bag and sealed it. The knife went into a companion bag.

"Don't get all huffy," Rose said indignantly. "My neighbor works in a bakery. A suspicious-looking guy with silver eyes came into the shop and bought a chocolate cake—a Black Forest cake, I think it's called. When she got home there was a slice of cake on the steps. The very same cake."

"How did she know it was the very same cake? Did the cake have fingerprints?"

"Very funny, Vincent," Rose said. "She sold the cake two hours ago. I think she can recognize it."

"Where is this slice of cake now?"

"My other neighbor, Murray Zimmerman, fed it to a squirrel."

"Ma," Vincent said patiently. "You realize this story is ridiculous."

"This story is not ridiculous!" Rose insisted. "There are the crumbs! There is the plate! There is the knife! You can interview my neighbors!"

"But Ma, there's no evidence that a crime was committed. Putting a slice of cake on somebody's steps is not a crime."

"Just talk to her," Rose said. "I think somebody is stalking her, and that would be a crime, wouldn't it?"

Vincent sighed. "Since I'm here, I'll talk to your neighbor. But I gotta tell you, you haven't convinced me this amounts to anything."

When Vincent reached Rose's apartment, Betsy was quietly drinking tea on the overstuffed side chair. She looked up and her jaw dropped.

"You're Mrs. B's Vincent?" she exclaimed.

"Guilty as charged. I remember you too. You're Betsy Mangero, the girl who stalked the musician."

"I did no such thing! I explained that to you."

"And I explained to *you*," Vincent said, "that you can't just take pictures of random people because you have a crush on them."

"He wasn't random," Betsy said. "He lived in my home town. He went to my church."

"But the point is, he didn't want you to take pictures of him, but you did it anyway. That's harassment."

"I wasn't harassing him. And the pictures I took weren't embarrassing. The selfie after the concert at Carnegie Hall— he let me take that. The rest of the time I just took pictures of him eating, or reading, or practicing his cello."

Rose sat down beside Betsy. "Would somebody please explain what you're talking about?"

Betsy sighed. "Remember I told you I liked Greg Thomas, Carl's roommate?"

"It sounds as if it might have been a little more than 'liked'," Vincent said.

"Really, Vincent," Rose said. "I don't see how that's a problem for the police."

Vincent turned to his mother. "Betsy took pictures of Greg on her cell phone without his permission and against his will. I explained to her that this was a misdemeanor. Which means it's against the law."

"Oh, for heaven's sakes!" Rose said.

Vincent turned back to Betsy. "But that's not our subject right now. What can you tell me about the man you saw in the bakery?"

"The serial killer? I think he should be pretty easy to spot," Betsy said. "He has silver eyes."

"You can buy those in a Halloween costume store. Or on the internet any time of year. They're contact lenses."

"No! Really?"

"Swear to God," Vincent said, raising his right hand. "Online, it's always Halloween."

Rose and Vincent waited politely as Betsy digested this. "Well," she said at last, "that will make him a little harder for you to track him down. I was so focused on his eyes that I didn't pay much attention to his other features. That's all I can tell you about him. I'm sorry."

Vincent looked at Rose, and then back at Betsy. "Did he threaten you in any way? Was he physically abusive to you? Did he steal any personal belongings, or shoplift anything at the bakery? Do you have another reason that we should be looking for this man? Because wearing contact lenses isn't a crime, and neither is buying a cake."

"But he's a serial killer!" Betsy cried. "He left a slice of cake and a knife on my steps to show that he wants to kill me!"

"What makes you think he's a serial killer?" Vincent asked.

"Carl warned me about serial killers," Betsy answered. "He said they prey on girls like me."

Vincent and Rose exchanged glances. "Well, I wouldn't worry too much about that," Vincent said. "Ma, could I have a word with you in the kitchen?"

"Anything you can say to me," Rose said stiffly, "you can say to Betsy."

"I'm sure that's true," Vincent agreed. "But indulge me."

He ushered Rose into the darkened kitchen and closed the door noiselessly behind them. "If you call me out to this building again," he hissed, "it had better be your birthday or Christmas. But it had better not have anything to do with Betsy Mangero, who is nuttier than a fruitcake."

"I'll grant you that she's not awfully bright," Rose said defensively, choosing to ignore all the times she pretended to be somewhere else when Betsy knocked on the door. "And I know she can be a little out there."

"Jupiter is out there. She's in a whole other solar system. I would be happy to give you a list of social service agencies who can deal with the mentally challenged. There are plenty of them in the county. But I am not one of them."

Rose opened her mouth to protest, but Vincent held up a warning finger. "Since I'm here," he said, "I will fill out an incident report. But I want you to know that I'm not really going to track down a guy with silver contact lenses who leaves cake on the front steps of a residential building."

"But—"

"No buts," Vincent said. "No buts at all."

He swung through the kitchen door, leaving his mother fuming at the stove. "Okay, Betsy!" he said heartily. "Let's write down the whole story of your mysterious encounter."

When Rose emerged from the kitchen with a reheated teapot, she found Vincent and Betsy sitting at the dining room table, their heads bent together over a notepad.

"He had a tan, or maybe just darker skin," Betsy said. "And he wore a hat like Humphrey Bogart in *The Maltese Falcon*. Cary Grant used to wear those hats a lot too. Come to think of it, his suit looked old-fashioned—like they went with the hat. And he had on thin, tight gloves. Like a doctor."

"We're still talking about the man in the bakery, right?" Vincent said. "Not Humphrey Bogart or Cary Grant? Because I don't remember them wearing latex gloves."

Betsy nodded vigorously. "Yes, the man in the store. He definitely had gloves."

"What did he do next?" he asked Betsy.

"The guy went back and forth and back and forth in front of the door," Betsy said. "For a really long time—maybe twenty minutes. At last he came in and he seemed like he was looking for something."

"Maybe he just couldn't decide what he wanted."

"No, it wasn't like that. He saw my phone on the counter, and he came over and swiped his fingers over the screen. Normally I don't let people touch my phone, but he looked so scary I was afraid to take it away from him. I asked if I could help him, and he told me he wanted the perfect cake for a lady. I showed him the Black Forest cake we had on display. He ran his tongue over his lips and said the cherry filling looked delicious, like blood. And all this time he was still swiping his fingers over my cell phone."

"There!" Rose said triumphantly. "Tell me that's not creepy."

"I just think it's weird," Vincent said. "What did he do after that?"

"After I boxed up the cake, he paid me."

"How did he pay you? Cash, check, credit card?"

"Cash. Two twenty dollar bills, and he didn't take the change. That alone should show you he was up to no good."

"It shows me he's not very thrifty," Vincent said. "Then he left?"

"Yes, thank God, and I picked up my phone and put it in my bra since Samantha wasn't there."

Vincent glanced over at his mother, who shrugged apologetically. He returned his attention to Betsy.

"And you never saw the guy again?"

Betsy shook her head, and Vincent leaned back in his chair with a sigh.

"Betsy," he said, "I know you think this incident is strange, but you're making a mountain out of a molehill. A man comes into a bakery to buy a cake. He buys the cake. He is attracted in some way to the girl who works in the bakery. He follows her home and leaves a slice of cake on the steps of her house. What am I missing?"

"He left me a knife," Betsy said. "And he got to my house before I did."

Vincent furrowed his eyebrows in thought, and then said, "Got it. Maybe this isn't the first time he's followed you. He already knew where you lived, just like you already knew where Greg and Carl lived."

"Well, I think that's even worse, don't you?" Betsy asked. "Wouldn't that make you really nervous?"

"Maybe you made Greg nervous when you did the same thing to him," Vincent said.

Rose kicked Vincent under the table. "Don't you have a card with your work number on it?" she asked him.

"*My* work number?" Vincent repeated.

"Of course," Rose said with a smile. "It's important to know that whenever there's a problem, the local police are at your service."

Vincent extracted his business card from his pocket and handed it to Betsy. "If anything else happens," he said between clenched teeth, "you call me. Especially if that guy comes back to the bakery, or you find any more slices of cake lying around in places they shouldn't be, or you see anybody suspicious hanging around the apartment."

"If anything else happens," Rose said, "you won't have to wait for Betsy to call you. I will."

"Somehow," Vincent said, "that wouldn't surprise me."

Chapter Four
Tuesday, February 3
3:25 p.m.

While Rose sorted laundry the next morning, she thought about the very strange events of the previous day. After Vincent had left, she and Betsy had talked for a long time. She'd learned that Betsy had moved to Binghamton about six months before, after having a falling-out with her older sister back home in Connecticut. She was a little vague as to why she'd chosen Binghamton, but Rose was pretty sure it had more than a little to do with Greg studying at Binghamton University.

She remembered Betsy's excitement when she got her job at the Cakery, but Rose now realized it was more than the prospect of earning a paycheck; many college students visited the Cakery for coffee and bagels, and Betsy could pass Greg's apartment every day on her way to and from work. While it would be very easy for Betsy to randomly pop in and out of Greg's pad, Rose doubted that she had actually done that often, if ever. Was there a time, Rose wondered, when Betsy and Carl and Greg had all been friends? If so, what had happened to change that?

Halfway up the basement steps, Rose heard the pounding of Betsy's feet above her. She set down the laundry basket and met a gasping Betsy at the back door.

"Mrs. B! He's dead! He crashed through the window and died!"

"Who died?" Rose asked. But since Betsy continued to charge up the steps toward her own apartment, Rose dashed after her. *"Who died?"*

"Carl!" Betsy cried, fumbling in her purse for her key. "He came out the window and smashed onto the street! He's dead, Mrs. B! Carl's dead!"

Murray Zimmerman's door opened and he shuffled toward them. "What's with the screaming already?" he asked.

"Betsy says there was an accident." Rose answered, reaching the door of her own apartment.

"It wasn't an accident!" Betsy protested. "He was pushed. Right out the window. Three stories up! That's how I know he's dead!"

"Who was pushed?" Murray asked. "What window? Did you see who did it? Did you call the police?"

A door opened and shut somewhere in the building, and Mr. Esposito's inquisitive head appeared on the landing. Giving up, Rose hauled Murray and Betsy into her apartment and closed the door firmly behind them.

"Everybody sit down!" she commanded. "Betsy, you take the loveseat."

The girl sat down on the plastic-covered cushion gingerly, as if she might damage it (which, Rose observed to herself, was impossible—that was the point of the plastic). Murray started to sit down on the loveseat beside Betsy, but Rose bumped him onto the side chair.

"Betsy, yes or no," she began. "You saw an accident, in Binghamton, on the way home from work, and it looked like somebody died."

Betsy started to embark on another tirade, but Rose raised her finger.

"Yes, you did see something, or no, you didn't see anything at all."

Betsy nodded vigorously. "Yes. I did."

"What did you see?"

"I saw Carl come out the window of his apartment and land in the street. When he was falling out the window, he was screaming, but when he landed on the pavement, he stopped screaming. When I looked again, his head was all bloody."

"Then I am calling Vincent," Rose said. She stood up to grab the handset of her cordless phone. "Vincent's my son," she told Murray. "He's a detective with the Binghamton police."

"It won't do any good," Betsy said. "And I'll just get in trouble."

"Why would you get in trouble?" Murray asked. "You didn't do anything wrong."

"But I did." Betsy turned all her attention toward Murray. "I was right outside their apartment. On Hesse Street. And I wasn't supposed to be."

"I'll hold," Rose told the voice on the other end of the phone.

"Right outside whose apartment?" Murray asked, reaching for a candy dish on the coffee table.

"Carl and Greg's. Carl was the one who died. Greg—" Betsy stood up, then flopped down again. "Somebody needs to tell Greg! But I can't do it."

Murray looked over at Rose. "Do you know what she's talking about?"

Rose held up a finger to silence Murray when her son came on the line.

"Detective unit, Bevelacqua," Vincent said.

"It's your mother. We have another situation with Betsy."

This verbal explosion was more than a sigh. "Ma, enough! We have a situation here too—a real one. A kid just jumped out a window—college student. Probably drunk or high, but I've got to go over and have a look."

"If it's on Hesse Street, his name is Carl, and Betsy's our witness."

"Seriously? Ma, we've discussed this. Betsy's not credible."

"You might change your mind after you talk to her," Rose said.

"I doubt it, but if you say she saw the guy jump, I'll be there as soon as I'm done at the crime scene."

As Rose hung up, Betsy leapt to her feet. "Look, I gotta go. He's just going to yell at me again."

"Why would he yell at you?" Murray asked.

Betsy began to sob. "Because I was on Hesse Street!"

Murray looked at Rose quizzically, and she said, "I suspect that a while back one of the boys who lived in the apartment on Hesse Street called the police to accuse Betsy of harassing him, and she's not too eager to get involved with the police again. Do I have that right?"

Betsy nodded, sniveling. "Your son doesn't have to tell me twice."

Rose restrained herself from saying that obviously he did, because telling her once had done no good.

"Betsy, could you tell me the whole story?" Murray asked. "Rosie, you make us some coffee."

Rose bristled on three different fronts: she hated being called Rosie, she hated being ordered around like the hired help in her own apartment, but most of all she hated being exiled from the center of the action.

"I don't do coffee," she said. "In my house we drink tea."

"Tea's fine," Murray replied amiably, never swerving his placid gaze from Betsy.

Not really feeling she'd won the battle, Rose hovered over the coffee table for a few minutes, and then finally went into the kitchen to put the kettle on. When she returned to the living room, she settled onto the sofa beside Betsy.

"I knew Greg from high school," Betsy was saying. "I'm not sure how he and Carl wound up living together on Hesse Street. You know—those two brick buildings right next to another?"

Rose knew which apartment buildings Betsy meant. They had probably been lovely mansions in the 1800s, but last year there had been a fire in one of them, and a few months later, a drug bust.

"Well, I work the register at the Cakery on Court Street. Carl and Greg used to come in a lot to get bagels, and Greg introduced me to Carl. I thought we were friends, and it was nice. I used to take pictures until Detective Bevelacqua said I couldn't do that anymore."

She pulled a thin phone from her cleavage, swiped her finger over its glassy surface, and tapped several times. Rose leaned in closer, and then closer still. She couldn't identify the subjects of the photographs, but most were definitely what her granddaughter Parker called "selfies"—close-ups of one person or a small, tightly-packed group.

"This is Greg," Betsy said sadly, and then sat bolt upright. "Oh, my God! You don't think Greg was in the apartment when Carl got pushed out the window? You don't think Greg is hurt, or they pushed him out the window too? Because if anything happened to Greg, I don't know what I'd do."

"I'm sure Greg is fine," Murray murmured, passing the candy a second time and taking some himself. "Do you have a picture of Carl?"

Betsy didn't seem interested in showing pictures of Carl. "Nobody understands," she moaned, her head drooping over her hands. "Mrs. B's son told me that Greg doesn't like it when I follow him around, and he could have me arrested. I know Greg would never do that—I'm from his home town. I went to his church."

"We get that," Rose said. "You knew him really well."

"So it hurts my feelings to know that he complained about me to a policeman. I would never hurt him in any way. I love him. I just want to know if he's home, or if he's at school, or if he's gone to bed, and I want to hear him play his cello—that's the best thing in the world. I went to see him perform in New York City—that was before he talked to the policeman about me—and we took this picture. See— here's Greg and me. Together."

Rose had leaned so far forward to see the pictures that the sudden shriek of the kettle in the kitchen almost knocked her to the floor. "Tea-time!" she called with false cheeriness, pushed herself to her feet, and quickly prepared three cups of steaming hot chamomile.

"Betsy, what did you do after you saw Carl fall?" Rose asked, setting a mug of tea on the marble table in front of her guest. "Did you go over and see if you could help him?"

"God, no!" Betsy looked incredulous. "His head was totally smashed in. There was blood all over the street. I didn't want to see, like, eyeballs and teeth. And I didn't want to go down Main Street because I thought that maybe the guy who pushed Carl had seen me standing on the corner. I cut around the back of the building and ran home. But now I'm wondering what if Greg was inside and I just ran off? Wouldn't that be leaving the scene of a crime?"

Murray leaned forward in his chair. "Are you sure you didn't see the guy who pushed Carl?"

Betsy started to shake her head, but then stopped. "I'd have to think," she said, as if this were a new experience for

27

her. "I don't remember seeing him. But I'm so sure Carl was pushed—I'd have to think."

"You do that. Me, I'm waiting for Vincent," Rose said, taking a sip from her mug. "Murder isn't really my cup of tea."

Chapter Five
Tuesday, February 3
3:55 p.m.

For way too long, Rose half-listened to Murray regale Betsy with stories of his childhood in the Williamsburg section of Brooklyn while she added fresh hot water to the teacups, refreshed the teabags, and took a roll of Thin Mints out of the freezer. At last she heard Vincent's characteristic rap on the door; a moment later, his head of dark curly hair appeared in the opening.

"Knock-knock," he said to his mom, and looked past her to her two guests.

Murray half-rose and extended a hand. "Murray Zimmerman. I live down the hall. In Joe Rossi's old apartment, may he rest in peace."

Rose crossed herself, and Betsy did too.

Vincent sat down on the arm of the couch and opened the little notebook he carried in his pocket. "Betsy, my mom said you observed an incident that occurred today on Hesse Street."

Betsy nodded, wringing her hands in her lap. "Carl came flying out of the window and landed in the street. It was awful."

"We're talking about Carl Feinstein, Greg Thomas' roommate?"

Betsy nodded again. "He was some kind of genius or something. Like the guys on *Scorpion*, but with math. Remember that show, *Numbers*?"

"I don't watch much TV," Vincent said, scribbling in his notebook. "How long had you known Carl?"

"Maybe six months—Greg introduced us." Betsy suddenly bounced to the edge of her seat. "Can you find out if Greg's okay? I'm just worried that the guy who pushed Carl out the window might have pushed Greg out too, or stabbed him or shot him or something. I just want to know he's all right. I don't want to bother anyone."

"She's a very caring person," Murray put in.

"I'm sure," Vincent replied, his eyebrows a straight line. "Right now, though, I'd like you to tell me about what you saw today at the apartment on Hesse Street. Because, even though I told you to stay away, you were there, weren't you?"

Betsy started to cry. "I didn't go inside, honest. I was on my way home from work and I just stopped on the corner to—to—"

"Watch the house?" Vincent finished, and Betsy broke out in a fresh wave of sobs.

"Betsy, for God's sake, spit it out. Vincent doesn't have all day." Rose pushed a box of tissues toward her.

Betsy honked her nose loudly and went on. "I was standing on the corner, across the street from their building. And all of a sudden, there was this huge crash. I looked up and Carl was falling through the air. Screaming. He came through the living room window, waving his arms like a lunatic. He flew over the sidewalk and into the street and his head split open like a coconut. Except bloodier. And then, of course, he wasn't screaming any more, but you wouldn't expect him to."

Vincent looked over at his mother; his eyebrows hiked upwards, and hers matched.

"So what did you do?" Vincent asked.

"Well, for a minute I just stood there," Betsy said. "It was exactly like *Bones*, except it wasn't on television. And then all of a sudden I realized that maybe the person who came after Carl would come after me. So I took the back way home because I was scared. That was thoughtless of me, though. I should have tried to find out if Greg was there. He could have been in danger."

"We have investigators down there right now," Vincent told her. "There were no other victims in the apartment."

"Did they find a piece of Black Forest cake anywhere near the body? Or a knife?"

Vincent stopped writing. "You think the guy who left the cake on your steps was the one who pushed Carl out the window."

"It's the only logical conclusion, isn't it? Carl was the one who told me about the serial killer in the first place," Betsy answered. "He hadn't phoned me since—well, you know, the whole thing with Greg calling the police on me a couple of weeks ago. But yesterday he called me at work—remember, I told you I was talking to Carl when the serial killer came. And he said there was a serial killer on the Binghamton University campus, and I ought to go visit my sister in Connecticut until they catch him. Carl said the serial killer has been stalking girls who were, you know, kind of curvy like me. Then he strangles them and leaves a piece of cake next to their bodies. I told you all this yesterday. Weren't you listening?"

"Apparently not," Vincent replied, stealing a look at his mom.

"Carl said that the reason nobody's heard about it is that the campus police force has hushed the whole thing up," Betsy continued. "It would make the college look bad."

"I'm sure it would," Vincent said, "but Betsy, I'm positive there is no serial killer on campus, and there never has been. The campus police couldn't have hushed that up if they wanted to, and trust me, they wouldn't want to. So there's nothing to cover up, and nothing for you to worry about. Really."

"Then why would Carl tell me there was?"

"That," said Vincent, "is a very good question."

"And the part about the cake doesn't make sense," Rose put in. "Why would this person leave a piece of cake in Carl's apartment? He said the serial killer was after curvy women. And obviously Carl was not a woman, curvy or otherwise."

"I wondered about that too, at first," Betsy said. "Not the cake, but why they would kill him. But then I figured it out. The serial killer had to kill Carl because Carl warned me about him. And I might talk to the police—oh, God. Look what I'm doing."

Murray reached over and took Betsy's hand. "You had to tell the police, Betsy. If you didn't, that would be disrespectful to Carl, and he was a good friend to you, wasn't he?"

Betsy's chin started to tremble again, and she nodded. "Greg is the one I love, but Carl was really sweet. Like Leonard on the *Big Bang Theory*."

Vincent flipped his notebook closed. "Well, Betsy, I really appreciate your help. Why don't you have some more tea and chat with Mr. Zimmerman while I talk to my mom in the kitchen?"

"Not again," Rose muttered.

"You asked for it," Vincent muttered back.

They went into the darkened kitchen and closed the door.

"Ma, I still can't use her testimony. She isn't any more rational than she was yesterday."

"Of course she isn't. But she has pictures."

"You mean the ones she took of Greg?"

32

"And probably Carl," Rose reminded him. "And if there are pictures of Carl and Greg, who knows what else there might be on her phone?"

"True." Vincent tapped his interview pad against the fingers of his other hand. "It's not much, but it's something. I'll have her send the photos downtown."

They went back out to join Betsy and Murray.

"Betsy," Vincent said, lapsing into his kindergarten-teacher voice, "we know you have pictures of Carl and Greg on your phone. It would help me to know what Carl looked like when he was alive, and what Greg looks like now. Could you send the pictures to me?"

"How would I do that?" Betsy asked, genuinely mystified.

"You don't know how to send photos from your phone?"

"I don't know how to do much of anything on my phone. My sister gave it to me when we were still speaking. All I know how to do is answer the phone, listen to messages, and take pictures."

"Can I take your phone for a minute?" Vincent asked, extending his hand.

"No!"

Her refusal was so abrupt and so unequivocal that everyone jumped.

"I told you," Betsy added. "I don't like anyone touching my phone."

"For God's sake, Betsy, give him the phone," Rose said. "He just wants to show you how to do something new."

"It's okay, Betsy," Murray said soothingly. "You can trust him."

Betsy shook her head. "I'm sorry. But no. Nobody can use my phone but me. Sometimes people take my phone and erase things by mistake, and then everything's gone forever."

An awkward silence filled the room. Finally Vincent said, "Suppose you hold the phone, and I just point to the places on the phone you could touch to send me the photo. Could we do that?"

Betsy contemplated this. "I guess that would be all right," she said at last.

Rose watched the interaction between her normally impatient son and the girl who required so much patience. Over Betsy's shoulder she saw a cuddly picture of Betsy and a handsome fair-haired man in a black tuxedo—this must be the Carnegie Hall shot of Greg that Betsy had mentioned earlier. There was a head shot of a studious-looking young man with thick-rimmed glasses, leaning against a bookcase—that must be Carl Feinstein.

Murray leaned forward, his finger hovering over the screen. "There is a haggadah on the bookshelf—an order of service for Passover," he added for Rose's benefit. "Was Carl very observant? Did he do a lot of things that struck you as Jewish?"

Betsy shook her head. "The book belonged to his grandfather. Carl wasn't religious at all."

Vincent uploaded eight or ten more pictures before Rose slipped a fresh mug of hot tea into Betsy's hands.

"There, you survived, right?" she said. "And your pictures are still on your phone, and you know how to do something you couldn't before."

"I guess," Betsy said, taking a long sip. "I'll probably forget, though. It doesn't seem like something I'd want to do very often."

Vincent gave his mother a very strange look before turning back to Betsy. "Now, I don't want you to think you're a suspect, but I'm going to have to ask you not to leave town until we've finished investigating Carl's death. We might need to talk to you again."

Betsy looked unsure. "Carl told me I had to leave town as soon as I could because the serial killer was after me," she told Vincent. "But now you say there isn't a serial killer, and I shouldn't leave town at all because the police might need to talk to me. If there isn't a serial killer, then staying here would be okay—but if there is, then staying here might kill me. So I think I'll go to Connecticut instead, if you don't mind."

The vein in Vincent's right temple throbbed. "I do mind," he said. "There is absolutely no serial killer, Betsy. Right now you are on my fifteenth nerve, and I don't have sixteen. If you leave town, I will have you arrested." He spun on his heel and left.

"What a putz!" Murray said.

Rose had no idea what a putz was, but it didn't sound complimentary. "Murray," she said, "Go home. Betsy and I need to chill out."

"I'm sorry I called your son a putz --"

"Just please go home."

Betsy sobbed for a few minutes after Murray left, and Rose resumed folding the laundry she'd begun hours before.

"Vincent can be a jerk, but he's right, you know," she said at last. "I don't know why Carl told you there was a serial killer, but there isn't. He just fell out the window, that's all."

"You didn't see him," Betsy sniffed.

"No, I didn't, but I'm pretty sure about this."

Betsy didn't answer; she sat so still on the couch that she reminded Rose of a mouse cowering in a corner. A small chunk of the ice in Rose's heart melted. "Betsy, do you want to stay for supper? Nothing fancy—maybe ham sandwiches—but you wouldn't have to eat alone when you're still so upset."

Betsy shook her head. "I'll be fine. I've got my cat, you know."

"Then at least come over for dinner tomorrow. My daughter Diane and my granddaughter Parker usually have dinner with me on Wednesday night. You'd be welcome to join us."

Betsy looked as if she was about to decline again, but instead she managed a small smile. "Can I bring dessert from the bakery?"

Rose put in a special request for Valentine butter cookies—her favorites. Sadly, her request was not to be fulfilled.

Chapter Six
Wednesday, February 4
5:13 p.m.

Rose, who was always punctual, had been cursed with a daughter who would turn up late to her own funeral and a teenage granddaughter who wasn't any better. She knew Diane's shift at the hospital ended at 3:00 p.m. and Parker got home from school a few minutes later, so there didn't seem to be any reason they couldn't make it ten miles to Rose's apartment by five. Nonetheless, they never seemed able to do that, so Rose invariably told them dinner was at 5 and planned it for 5:30.

At 5:13, the macaroni and cheese was starting to bubble, so Rose popped the garlic bread into the oven and gave the salad a vigorous spin. None of her dinner guests had arrived, and while she wasn't worried about Diane or Parker, she had an unsettling concern about Betsy, whom she'd invited to dinner the same night. Betsy wasn't the quietest of apartment dwellers, and Rose often heard her clunking heavily up the stairs, or rattling her noisy assortment of keyfobs against the brass door handle, or scolding the cat for escaping into the hallway when his owner came home. Today Rose had heard Betsy leave for work at six in the morning, and hadn't heard another sound since.

The macaroni and cheese was out of the oven, the salad was on the table, and the garlic bread was turning golden brown when Parker and her mother burst in.

"Jeepers Cats!" Parker exclaimed, stomping her feet and shaking the snow off her parka. "It's got to be thirty degrees below zero out there!"

"And this is why you dump snow in my house?" Rose asked. "Take your boots off in the hallway. Nobody will steal them. And drape your wet coat on the chair over there."

Diane shook the snowflakes from her short blond highlights and produced two bottles from an insulated tote. "Don't worry—one of these is nonalcoholic. The other one's for me."

"Behave yourself," Rose said severely, and her daughter just laughed. Diane was Rose's oldest child, perky and ever-confident, and just as gifted a nurse as Vincent was a detective. The loss of Rose's third child, Anthony, made her treasure her two remaining children and her granddaughter all the more. And it made her worry about all the lost children of the world, which was why her mind again turned to Betsy. Why was she so late?

Rose let Parker demonstrate all the features of her new cell phone, pretending to be fascinated. In truth she could not imagine why anyone would want to waste their time and intelligence on such a ridiculous pastime. Parker showed her grandmother Facebook, asserting that she could find out about "practically anybody," just by typing in their name.

"Put in Betsy Mangero," Rose told her.

"Your neighbor?" Diane asked, gingerly dropping the hot garlic bread into a napkin-lined basket. "Is she the one you invited to dinner?"

"You can't find her that fast," Parker said. "I mean, there would probably be more than one Betsy Mangero, so you'd have to figure out which one you're looking for, and that might take a while, and she may not have made all her photos public—"

"I don't think Nonni wants to know all that, Park," Diane said gently. She put her arm around Rose's shoulders. "You're worried about Betsy, right?"

Rose nodded. "She keeps a really regular schedule, like I do," she told her daughter. "She comes home the same time every day. She doesn't go out much, and if she does, she usually tells me where she's going, even if I don't particularly care. She'd promised to come over for dinner tonight, and she seemed pleased when I asked her—she was going to bring cookies from the bakery where she works. Something is wrong—I can feel it."

"Maybe she came home really quietly and she's taking a nap," Parker suggested. "I do that a lot after school. Do you want me to go knock on her door?"

"I'll go," Rose said. "You guys set the table. And if she's not home, we'll just eat. The garlic bread will get cold if we wait any longer."

"Sounds good to me!" Parker said cheerfully, but Diane shot her a warning look.

Rose crossed the hall and rapped quietly on Betsy's door. She didn't hear any answer, so she knocked a little louder.

"Betsy? You there?" she asked. Inside, she heard Betsy's cat yowling for his supper. "Betsy?"

Predictably, Murray's door opened. Today he was wearing a blue striped shirt and a red bow tie. "Isn't she home?" he asked.

"I don't think so," Rose answered.

"What did you need her for?"

Rose sighed inwardly. Being Italian, she'd made plenty of food, and she was apparently going to be short one dinner guest.

"I'd invited her for dinner," she said. "We've got plenty. Would you like to come?"

Murray's eyes brightened. "I wouldn't want to impose," he said.

"You're not imposing. My daughter and granddaughter are visiting, and I'm sure they'd love to see you."

They went back across the hall into Rose's cheerful kitchen. "No Betsy, but I brought another guest. Murray Zimmerman, you've met my daughter, Diane McCarthy?"

"Hi, Mr. Zimmerman," Diane said brightly. "How nice to see you! This is *my* daughter Parker. Have a seat next to me."

They sat down at Rose's small rectangular kitchen table with Parker and Rose on one side and Diane and Murray on the other. Murray beamed as he looked over the bubbling pan of macaroni and cheese, the colorful salad, and the steaming garlic bread.

"We normally say grace," Rose said. Diane and Parker both looked up in surprise, since they never said grace except at Christmas or Thanksgiving.

"Oh, that's fine," Murray said. "Do whatever you normally do."

Rose composed herself, made the sign of the cross, and opened one eye to make sure Diane and Parker did the same. "Bless us, oh Lord, and these thy gifts which we are about to receive from thy bounty, through Christ our Lord."

All the women said "Amen," and crossed themselves again. Rose looked up, satisfied with her demonstration of piety.

Smiling, Murray took a chunk of garlic bread from the basket and added, "As it happens, I also have a blessing for bread."

"Really?" Diane said, her gaze shifting mischievously toward her mother. "Please share it with us. My mother is always eager to learn new things."

Everyone closed their eyes and folded their hands except for Murray, who turned his palms heavenward. "Blessed are

40

you, Lord our God, King of the universe, who brings forth bread from the earth. Amen."

"You know what?" Parker said. "That was probably what Jesus said at Passover. That's cool. Thanks, Mr. Zimmerman!"

"You can eat all this, can't you?" Diane asked. "I mean, being Jewish. This meal is meatless, so there's no problem, right?"

"It's much more complicated than that," Murray said, "but the short answer is, I no longer keep kosher. When I ran the furniture store, I went to a lot of luncheon meetings and dinners, and I found it impossible to keep kosher in a secular community. So I have to confess I gave it up, first when I was out of the house, and then altogether when Reva died. My son David disagrees with me, but I'm free to make my own choices as he's free to make his. I am still faithful in my attendance at temple, and I still keep the Sabbath the way I always have. But I don't keep kosher—so yes, this meal is just fine."

Everyone took a big helping of macaroni and cheese, salad, and garlic bread.

"So what do you think's keeping Betsy?" Murray asked, digging his fork into his supper.

Parker looked at Diane, who looked at Rose, who looked down at her napkin.

"We don't know," Diane said at last. "My mom is worried. She doesn't like to admit it— "

"I don't mind admitting it!" Rose protested. "Just because Betsy annoys me doesn't mean I can't worry about her. She promised to come, and I just can't see her forgetting about it."

"Maybe she had a better offer," said Parker.

"Better than this?" Murray gestured at his plate with a fork. "Impossible. You have every right to worry. She's had a rough few days."

"Why? What happened to her?" Diane asked. "Spill the beans."

Rose took a deep breath. "Yesterday a good friend of Betsy's jumped out a window and was killed."

"Oh, right!" Parker said. "I saw that on the news. That was her friend?"

Rose nodded. "As far as we know, Betsy was the only witness. But the day before he died, this same guy had told Betsy there was a serial killer on the university campus and she was a likely target. He told her that the killer always left a slice of cake by the body."

Diane frowned. "Wait a minute. I don't remember seeing anything about a serial killer on the news."

"That's because there isn't any serial killer," Rose interjected. "Vincent checked it out. We're not sure why Betsy's friend made up that story. But the point is, Betsy believed it. So the day before yesterday she came home from work all upset, convinced that she'd met the serial killer. She said he came into the bake shop where she works and bought a cake."

"So he bought a cake," Diane said. "That's why they have bakeries."

"Apparently this guy looked extremely creepy, talked about blood, played with Betsy's phone, and made her nervous. And when she closed up the bakery at the end of the day, she found a slice of the cake she'd just sold him on our front steps."

Parker dropped her fork. "These front steps? Of this house here?"

Diane stopped eating as well. "Oh, Mom, that's—troubling."

"Call Uncle Vincent," Parker urged. "Find out if he knows where Betsy is now."

"I'm not sure Uncle Vincent could tell you anything," Diane said. "Mom, do you know if she was in her apartment this morning?"

"She was," Rose said. "I heard her talk to the cat."

"Then it's too early to report her as a missing person. And if you called the hospital, the HIPAA laws would prevent them from telling you if she'd been admitted. The only thing you could definitely find out is if she were—"

Parker finished the thought no one wanted to say. "Dead."

"That's not possible," Rose said. "She can't be dead. Vincent would have called me."

So she called Vincent.

"Ma." Her son was clearly losing his patience. "I have not had any further developments on the Feinstein case, other than the fact that his parents have hired a lawyer to prevent an autopsy because they want to get the guy in the ground zippety-quick. And I have no idea where Betsy could be, although you know I asked her not to leave town. Maybe she went to the grocery store. Or the movies. Maybe she met the guy of her dreams and got lucky."

The guests at Rose's dinner party were not satisfied with that suggestion. No one wanted to say so, but they were all afraid that Betsy had gotten very unlucky indeed.

Chapter Seven
Thursday, February 5
8:00 a.m.

The first thing Rose heard when she woke up on Thursday morning was Betsy's cat, Daniel Striped Tiger. Rose had only been inside Betsy's apartment once, when Betsy had gone to Greg's concert in New York City, and that was the only time Rose had met the cat. But there was no question that the sound that awakened her today was one very distressed feline. Quickly Rose threw on her bathrobe and knocked on Betsy's door again. No answer, except for the yowling cat.

Rose hurried back into her apartment and scrounged through the kitchen junk drawer for a pair of paper clips. As she returned to the outside hallway, she straightened out one loop on both clips, and quickly inserted them into the keyhole of Betsy's door, jiggling them one way and another until the door opened.

"Well, hello again, Daniel," she said to the cat, bending over and picking him up. He broke into a loud spate of purring, nuzzling himself down into her neck. "Remember me? I'm the nice lady who fed you at Christmastime. Didn't Mama come home last night? Can I come in and see?"

She wandered into the darkened and deserted apartment, noting approvingly that even though Betsy hadn't expected company, the rooms were very neat. She flipped on the kitchen light and saw empty food and water bowls on the floor near the sink.

"I see your problem," she murmured. "Let's look around and see if we can't find some way to fix that."

Daniel continued to snuggle and purr as Rose opened one cabinet door after another. Betsy didn't own many dishes, and her larder was fairly bare as well; Rose felt a twinge of guilt for the many times she could have invited Betsy for dinner, and had not. Finally she found a package of cat food, and Daniel began to squirm delightedly as she filled his bowl.

"Don't eat too fast now," she admonished him. "You'll get sick, and cleaning up after you is not in my job description."

While Daniel gobbled his food, she took a moment to glance around the apartment. There was no indication she'd been planning to go away; all the clothes Rose had ever seen her wear still hung in the closet, there was a prescription bottle on the kitchen table—antibiotics, only two left—and a stamped utility bill lay on the counter, its check undoubtedly inside. And on the end table in the living room, a picture frame Rose had cavalierly given Betsy at Christmastime prominently displayed a photo of Greg and Betsy cheek-to-cheek. Rose was touched; the frame obviously meant more to the recipient than the giver.

When Daniel had finished his breakfast, augmented by a cool drink of water—he apparently preferred to drink straight from the faucet—Rose prepared to take her leave. Daniel wrapped himself around her ankles again.

"Oh, all right," Rose told him. "But if you're coming to my house, we're going to have to make some preparations."

She'd seen his litter box and an unopened container of litter in the bathroom, so she went to get them. The box turned out to be much heavier than she'd anticipated, and it required a considerable amount of muscle power to get it out of the bathroom, into the living room, and across the hall toward her own apartment. She was hunched over the box, dragging it along the carpeted floor when she sensed someone standing above her.

"Murray Zimmerman! You scared me half to death!"

"Might I ask what you're doing?" Today he had on a yellow shirt, red suspenders, and a blue and white polka-dot bow tie, which made him look like a kindergarten crayon box.

Rose gave him an exasperated look. "I'm moving a litterbox from one apartment to another, if you must know."

"I take it Betsy did not come home?"

"No."

"And you don't think she ever will?"

That idea hadn't fully formed in Rose's mind, and she pushed it out as soon as it went in. "This thing is heavy, and it smells. Are you going to help me or not?"

Murray hoisted the litter box into his arms and moved toward the door a little shakily. "You grab the container of litter and get the door. Do you think, if we leave the door open, the cat will follow us or run away?"

"Only one way to find out."

Daniel, being an intelligent cat who knew where his bread was buttered, serenely followed them into Rose's apartment.

"You stay here," Rose said to Murray as much as Daniel. "I've got to go get the bag of cat food and the bowls. Then I'll lock the apartment up again."

"I didn't know you had a key."

"I don't," said Rose, halfway out the door. "I have paper clips."

Murray's eyebrows hiked. "You must have an extremely interesting background."

Back in her own apartment, she pointed Murray in the direction of the bathroom. "When Anthony was three or four, he used to turn the little button on the back of the doorknob and then slam the door. The first couple of times he did it, I whacked his bottom and put him in time out. After that, I learned to pick locks."

Murray set the litter box down on the tile floor and followed Rose into the kitchen. "You do know that if there was a crime committed in Betsy's apartment, you've just contaminated the crime scene. To say nothing of breaking and entering."

"Fine," Rose said. She found a place for Daniel's food right next to her cereal. "You sit here and listen to that poor cat yowling all night and day as he slowly starves to death."

"I'm not saying that what you did was a bad idea. It was a mitzvah for the cat, but not so much for the police."

"Right now the police are not high on my list."

Murray sat down at the kitchen table. "Your son is a detective in the BPD."

"My son is not high on my list."

"So you think something's happened to Betsy?"

Rose sank into a kitchen chair. "Frankly, I do." She waved her hand in the general direction of Betsy's apartment. "You don't go off and just leave your cat. If you've taken nine days of an antibiotic, you finish off the bottle. You pack, for God's sake, and you put your bills in the mailbox. Something happened between Tuesday night when she was all upset about the serial killer at the bake shop and last night when she didn't come home."

Hearing the anxiety in Rose's voice, Daniel jumped up into her lap and she began to stroke him absentmindedly.

"When Anthony died—"

Murray sat down and put his hand over hers. "I didn't know your Anthony. But Betsy isn't Anthony, and I'm not sure this is a place that you want to go right now."

Shaking her head, Rose pulled her hand away. "What if Betsy's all alone? What if she's in trouble, and can't let anybody know?"

"Why couldn't she let anybody know?" Murray asked reasonably. "She's got a phone."

"I know. I don't understand it either. She must have known we'd worry."

Murray tapped the surface of the table. "Listen. You get yourself dressed, and we'll go out for breakfast."

"Breakfast?" Rose's voice rose to a shriek, and Daniel jumped off her lap in alarm. "I can't eat breakfast. I'm much too upset to eat breakfast!"

"I know you are," Murray said. "And you're much too upset to be sensible. Let's go to the Northside Diner, have some breakfast, and we'll figure out where to go from here."

Murray waited for Rose to get dressed, brush her teeth, and run a comb through her short grey hair. Then, on the way out, Rose slipped a note under Betsy's door that said, "Don't worry. Daniel is with me. Everything is fine."

She wished she felt as confident as that note implied.

*   *   *

At the Northside Diner, Murray ordered two eggs over easy, hashbrown potatoes, and two slices of rye toast. Rose ordered the same thing since she was going to pay for her own meal; if Murray paid it would feel like a date, and she didn't date—and if she did, she certainly wouldn't date anyone who wasn't Catholic. Nevertheless, at the Northside Diner the food was inexpensive and good and there was always plenty of coffee and tea, so Rose knew she and Murray could stay there a good long time.

"So we know," Murray said, pushing his empty cup to the table's edge so the server could fill it, "that Betsy was basically okay when she left your place on Tuesday night."

"Correct," Rose agreed. "She was upset about the strange customer at the bakery and upset about Carl, but she definitely did not give me the idea she was planning to take off in the middle of the night."

"Well, she didn't take off in the middle of the night, did she? She talked to the cat in the morning. At six o'clock—what did she say, do you remember?"

Rose thought. "She might have said 'Get back in here. You're not going anywhere'—something like that."

"Are you sure it was Betsy who said that?" Murray asked. "For instance, it wasn't another woman saying that to Betsy?"

"You mean, someone who had her at gunpoint and didn't want her to move?"

"Something like that."

Rose shook her head. "No, it was Betsy. That was the sort of thing she always said to the cat."

Murray thought a while longer. Suddenly he brightened. "You said she had prescription tablets."

"She took all of them but two. And then she left the rest of the bottle."

"Maybe they caused hallucinations. Maybe she didn't know where she was, and she's out wandering the streets somewhere, lost."

"Murray, stop it," Rose said. "They were just antibiotics, probably for a UTI. I've taken them a lot."

"But do they have delusions as a possible side effect? Especially if you combined them with another medication," Murray leaned back in his chair triumphantly.

"That would be something to check with Diane," Rose admitted.

"But even if she was delusional, that doesn't explain everything," Murray said. "For example, somebody really did leave a piece of cake on the steps. When I went downstairs to get the plate, the squirrel had eaten most of it, but there were still a few chocolate crumbs and a schmear of cherry filling."

"And a very long knife," Rose added. "And Carl really did fall out the window backwards, which isn't something you'd do if you lost your balance cleaning the glass."

"Another thing." Murray snapped his fingers. "If you dropped, say, a television set out a window, where would it land?"

Rose looked puzzled. "On the ground."

"But on the sidewalk, or in the street? Would it go straight down or arc outwards?"

"On the sidewalk. It would go straight down."

Murray looked triumphant again. "But where would it land if you put some force behind it and actually threw it out the window?"

Rose gasped. "In the street, which is where Betsy said Carl landed! She said it over and over again—'in the street, in the street.' Murray Zimmerman, you're a genius!"

"I have my moments," said Murray modestly. "I think, if you really want to find out what happened to Betsy, we're going to need to go out and ask some questions. Betsy's co-workers. Students or staff at the university. Even Greg. I'm not sure what kind of questions we would ask—"

50

"Easy," said Rose. "We could tell them that Betsy didn't come home last night and we were wondering if anybody knew where she went, because somebody's got to feed her cat."

Rose and Murray both sat back, satisfied. It was remarkable, Rose mused, how three good cups of tea and a couple of eggs can change one's outlook on life.

Chapter Eight
Thursday, February 5
10:00 a.m.

The Cakery was located on the north side of Court Street, in a building that had seen a great deal of change. A century ago, Binghamton was dubbed the Parlor City for all the elegant homes that graced its tree-lined streets; its downtown area was bustling with shops and banks and services catering to the affluent residents of those homes. The entire region thrived in the early 20th century due to industries such as IBM, Endicott-Johnson, Ansco and Link Aviation, and the block that would eventually house the Cakery catered to the wives of upscale businessmen. In the late 1900s, though, the companies that had once been the lifeblood of the area downsized, transferred workers to other locations, or closed entirely, and the windows of Court Street looked out on the unemployed, the insecure, the lost.

But as the 21st century dawned, nearby Binghamton University spread outside its suburban campus and established a dominant presence in the city. Now most of the people seen walking down Court Street's wide sidewalks were office workers or college students, and as a result, the Cakery—which had originally been established to bake custom wedding cakes for a high-society clientele—baked significantly fewer cakes and expanded its menu to offer lattes, bagels and muffins.

When Murray and Rose opened the door of the Cakery, they were still psyched from their conversation at the Northside Diner. At ten a.m., the Cakery should have been enjoying its mid-morning lull, but something was obviously wrong. The man running the register was wearing bakers' whites and a Carhartt jacket. A woman wearing an apron over a boho flowered skirt was speaking anxiously on the phone. The display case, which should have been full of scones, bagels, crullers and cupcakes, was half empty; through the open door to the kitchen, it was possible to see many of those goodies still spread out on baking trays.

As the last customer left, the man in the Carhartt jacket gestured helplessly to the woman on the phone. "Eileen? Eileen, I've got to go. I can't miss my bus—I have an exam today."

She put her hand over the receiver. "I'm taking a big order. Can you stay one more minute?"

"Honest, I can't. The bus will be coming by any second and I'm going to have to flag it down as it is." He hoisted a backpack from beneath the counter and ran past Rose and Murray, jangling the bell over the door as he left.

The only remaining employee smiled tautly at Rose and Murray, her fingertips still covering the receiver. "I'm sorry we haven't gotten our baked goods in the display case yet, and some things aren't decorated. But everything is baked. Give me a second and I'll show you what we— Excuse me." She quickly switched roles, speaking into the phone again. "Absolutely. So that's ten dozen Valentine butter cookies on the thirteenth, delivered. We can bring them in boxes, or there's a small additional upcharge if you want them plated. Absolutely. Absolutely. Got it. Thank you so much for your order, and for your patience today."

Murray smiled sympathetically as she hung up. "You sound overwhelmed."

"You have no idea." She ran a hand encircled by jangling gold bracelets through her curly hair. Her outfit simultaneously screamed "artist" and "rich." "The owner of the shop is at a Chamber of Commerce trade show, our baker has to leave precisely at ten to catch the bus to the university, and the employee who normally handles the register isn't here today, so we're a little short-handed to say the least."

"Did your missing employee call in sick?" Rose asked.

"Our missing employee just didn't show up. You don't know anyone who wants a job, do you?"

Rose had a feeling the woman wasn't kidding. "To be perfectly honest, that's why we're here. Not that we want a job, but Betsy is our neighbor. We invited her for dinner last night and she didn't come."

The woman frowned. "So what does that have to do with me?"

Murray suddenly extended his hand. "I'm sorry, we should have introduced ourselves. I'm Murray Zimmerman and this is my neighbor, Rose Bevelacqua. And you're—?"

Rose looked up at him in astonishment. In the blink of an eye, this was no longer a doddering old man with funky bow ties and suspenders. This was a confident professional with social skills.

"Eileen Reeves," the woman answered, returning Murray's handshake and reaching for Rose's hand as well.

"We're concerned that Betsy may be in trouble," Rose said. "She definitely didn't come home last night, and she's normally very predictable in her habits."

"That's for sure," Eileen said, and then backpedaled. "What I meant to say was—she—always arrived on time."

"Ms. Reeves," Murray began charmingly.

"Eileen, please."

"Eileen. We all want to make sure that Betsy has not been the victim of foul play, isn't that true? So why don't you tell us what you really meant to say?"

Eileen sighed. "Aside from her punctuality, which really was her greatest asset, all you could count on Betsy to do was everything wrong. She couldn't tell a cupcake from a muffin or a scone from a turnover. She asked people if they wanted cream cheese with their donut. Each of the items is clearly marked on the cash register—all you need to do is press the right button—but you do have to be able to identify the item, and she couldn't. I think it was part of her disability."

She said the word "disability" as if it were a heinous character defect.

"Do you normally have cakes all made up in advance, or do you bake and decorate them to order?" Murray asked.

Eileen smiled at her guilty secret. "Justin likes to bake cakes and I like to decorate them. So usually we'll bake two a day—maybe a coconut cake and a Black Forest, or a Devil's food and a lemon—and put them on display. By the end of the day, they're almost always gone. If they're not, we box them up for the staff and they take them home the next day. But that doesn't happen very often, or we'd go out of business."

"Have you given them to the staff recently?" Rose asked.

"No, we've sold out every day for a couple of weeks. What is this? Why do you care what we do with our cake?"

Rose and Murray exchanged glances. "No reason, really," Rose said.

Murray smiled broadly. "Betsy worked Tuesday alone, I believe."

"Probably. I think Samantha, the shop owner, was going to set up for the Chamber trade show after lunch, and I left not long after Justin did—my breakfast didn't agree with me, and I didn't even make it to the Arts Council. That's my primary job; I curate many of the exhibitions. Decorating cakes is just something I do as a favor to Samantha."

"Well, you must be good at it," Rose said.

Eileen patted her hair again. "Well, I like to think I am. Samantha's original designer left last year, and there was no way Samantha could entrust cake decorating to Betsy."

"So Betsy was left alone on Tuesday?" Rose said, trying to steer Eileen back to the original conversation.

"I don't see why that's your concern."

"Betsy came home very upset," Rose explained. "She told us that a man had come into the bakery and bought a Black Forest cake. He was strange-looking, he made her very nervous, and he told her the cherry filling looked like blood."

At first Eileen looked surprised, then she threw back her head and laughed. "And she thought he was a serial killer, right? All Tuesday morning, she went on and on about a serial killer at the university. My husband Brian is a highly-esteemed professor there, and I'm sure I don't have to tell you that last year Binghamton University was ranked 36th in top public schools by *US News and World Reports*. After my husband's last book came out, he was recruited by some of the best schools in the country, and chose Binghamton because of its stellar reputation. Trust me, there is no serial killer on *this* campus. Unless he kills cats."

"Cats?" Rose asked.

Eileen waved the idea away with a jingle of her bangle bracelets. "Yesterday morning Justin went out into the alley to put out some trash, and right outside the back door of the shop, he found a dead cat curled around a takeout box. There was a slice of cake inside."

Murray's nostrils flared just the tiniest bit. "Could we see the cat?"

"It's in the dumpster," Eileen said. "Now if that's all, I have to get back to work."

"Of course you do," Murray said smoothly. "Just a few more questions, and then we'll stop taking up your time. Did you notice that Betsy had many friends? Maybe people who came into the shop to see her, or people she met for lunch?"

"I really don't pay the least bit of attention to her friends," Eileen said. "I doubt she had any. She had a bad crush on a grad student in the music department, but I think it embarrassed him so he stopped coming in. Samantha told me the police warned Betsy that if she didn't leave the student alone, she'd be arrested for harassment. Betsy wasn't exactly attractive, you know. She always ate alone, in the back room, using her phone."

"Using it to do what?" Rose asked.

"Swiping her finger across it—I don't know. You know girls. They're all obsessed with Twitter and Instagram. Although what Betsy would have to tweet, I have no idea."

Murray thanked her. "We've taken up too much of your time, and I do apologize. But you've been very helpful. Could we have a plastic bag for the cat, in case we decide to take it with us?"

He smiled in the most disarming way, and Eileen dimpled, patting her curly hair. She knelt behind the counter and extracted a handful of plastic bags. "You might want more than one. I think it's sweet that you're playing detective to track Betsy down, but honestly, dead cats are above and beyond the call of duty."

"*Playing*? We are not playing—" Rose began hotly, but Murray quickly steered her out the door and around the building to the alley.

"Let go of me!" Rose bristled. "Miss High-and-mighty there, whose husband is a highly-esteemed professor at the university, can just go—"

But Murray had already flipped over a recycling bin to use as a stool and was pawing through the top layer of trash in the dumpster.

"Maggots," he said calmly. "Decent size. This cat didn't die yesterday. Found the cake box too. Black Forest. No knife."

Rose tried not to look until the rustling of plastic bags had stopped and the dumpster lid slammed shut. Then she watched Murray carefully lower himself off the recycling bin, holding a bundle securely wrapped in plastic.

"You're not putting that thing in the car with me," she said flatly.

"Rosie, it's my car," Murray pointed out. "You don't have a car, so you don't get to decide what I put in mine. But no worries—I'm putting the cat in the trunk. I want Levi to take it to school and get his forensics teacher's opinion. I'm curious to know how and when this cat died."

Levi, Rose knew, was Murray's grandson, a sophomore in the same high school that Parker attended. But whereas Murray seemed confident that Levi would be fascinated by the maggots on dead cats, she was equally confident that Parker wouldn't have shared the same opinion.

However, Parker would definitely be able to help her with another question, so Rose decided to make up a pan of baked ziti—Parker's favorite—and tap into her granddaughter's mastery of popular technology.

Chapter Nine
Thursday, February 5
5:30 p.m.

"I hope you didn't have anything else planned for dinner," Rose said, standing on the doorstep of Diane's rented duplex with a casserole dish in her hands. She knew that unless Diane had picked up a pizza on the way home from the hospital or grabbed a sub on the way to one of Parker's activities, there was no way she had anything planned for dinner.

Diane took the pan of cold ziti from her mother's hands as if it were a gift from the Magi, carried it reverently to the kitchen, and flipped the dial on the oven to 350°.

"You brought this all the way down on the bus?" Diane asked. "I'm sorry, I don't have salad or anything—"

Rose waved Diane's protests away. "I put bell peppers, mushrooms, and spinach in the ziti," she said. "And tomatoes, of course—that's plenty of veggies. You do have bread?"

Parker looked even more apologetic than Diane had. "Only whole wheat."

Rose considered for a moment. On the one hand, she'd rather eat ground glass than whole wheat bread. On the other, she really needed Parker's help. "Well, that will have to do," she said with unnatural cheerfulness.

"Okay, Mom, what do you want?" Diane asked.

Rose's hand flew to her bosom. "*Me*? I want nothing but to bring my favorite girls their favorite dinner."

"Baloney. You had us for dinner last night," her daughter pointed out, standing in front of the open refrigerator. "And

you hate whole wheat bread. You want something. —
Snapple?"

"Snapple would be lovely," Rose said, and meant it. "If
you have peach—"

"I do." Diane selected three bottles and joined Rose and
Parker at the bar. "Now spill it. My heart can't take the
suspense."

Rose went over her interviews at the Cakery. "So, bottom
line, I realized I can approach all these people cold, without
knowing anything about them, or I can do a little homework
first. For example, Parker, you were showing me how you
could look up practically anybody on Facebook and Google,
but then we got sidetracked and we never did it. Could you
show me now?"

"Sure," Parker said, extracting a tablet from the backpack
slung over her chair. She turned the tablet on and angled it so
Rose could see it. "You wanted to look up Betsy, right? And
you said her last name was—Moreno?"

"Mangero."

"Okay." Parker's Facebook app opened up on the screen
and a little keyboard appeared across the bottom. Parker
typed "Betsy Mangero" and frowned. "Hmm. There aren't
any Betsy Mangeros."

"What does that mean?" Rose wanted to know.

"It means she has an unusual name, but it also means that
Betsy doesn't have a Facebook account, unless she used a
different name when she registered with Facebook."

"Try Elizabeth Mangero." Seeing Parker's puzzled look,
she added "Betsy is a nickname for Elizabeth."

Parker's fingers flew over the tablet's glassy surface and
she shook her head. "Nope. Let me try Mangero with no first
name."

She repeated the exercise and exhaled. "No Betsy or Elizabeth—not many Mangeros at all—but there's a Sara Mangero in Litchfield, Connecticut. Would you like to look at her?"

"Definitely. Betsy said she had a sister in Connecticut, and both she and Greg came from there."

Parker clicked, and the image of a pretty girl appeared on the screen. This was what Betsy could look like, Rose thought, if she spent any time on herself. Sara had glossy dark hair, enormous brown eyes, and luminous skin. She wore a rose-colored top with a sweetheart neckline and a chunky necklace of semi-precious stones. But in bone structure and coloring, the resemblance to Betsy was unmistakable.

"That's her," Rose said. "That's Betsy's sister."

"Okay," Parker said. "Let's try something." Her fingers danced across the screen. "You lucked out because she has a business site. She's an artist. A lot of people make their personal sites private because they don't want strangers to find out too much about them. I do, because Mom insists on it, and it's safer. But if you have a business, you want strangers to contact you, right? So it's more open. Sara may have a personal site too, but at least by going into her business site, you can find out a little bit about her and how to get in touch. You can also find other people who have liked her site."

"It tells you that?" Rose asked in surprise.

"Sure. Do any of these people look familiar?"

Out of the string of photos flashing past her eyes, Rose picked out Greg and Carl.

Parker nodded approvingly. "That's good, because Greg Thomas is such a common name that if you'd gone looking for him the way we went looking for Betsy, you never would have found the right one. Let's click on his picture and look at his page." She tapped and then pointed at the screen. "There. That's what I meant by having a private page. Greg doesn't want to divulge too much information to people he doesn't know. So it says 'To see what he shares with friends, send him a friend request.' Then, if he accepts you, you're in. If he ignores your request or deletes it, you're not."

"So you couldn't find out any more about Greg without befriending him?" Rose asked.

"Friending," Parker corrected. "You can, but you have to use a tool other than Facebook. Let's go to Google."

Her flying fingers produced a number of blue-lined links spilling down the page, together with photos. "Greg is a cello player," she began.

"Cellist," Diane suggested.

"Cellist," Parker agreed. "He went to college in Connecticut, graduated come loud, whatever that means—"

"Cum laude," her mother said, pronouncing it correctly. "With honors. Not high honors, but nothing to sneeze at."

"Anyway," Parker continued, "he graduated last year. Now he's at Binghamton University and plays in the university symphony, which is having their next concert a week from Saturday with Greg as a featured soloist. And he's also played with other orchestras—wow, at Christmastime he performed at Carnegie Hall."

"You got all that from typing in his name?" Rose asked.

"Pretty much. I actually put in 'Greg Thomas Binghamton University,' and then I took the most likely results and clicked on them to get fuller answers. Pretty basic, really. I haven't done anything complicated."

"Let's go back to Carl Feinstein," Rose said. "What can you tell me about him?"

Again, the pads of Parker's fingers danced over the tablet screen. "Not as much," she admitted. "Last spring he got an award for research in computer science—"

"Wait," Rose interrupted. "Not math?"

"His undergraduate degree was in math. Same college, BU. He changed to the computer science department for graduate school. I guess he was really good in both of them."

"Definitely no moss growing on Carl, either," Diane mused.

"But there's not much else," Parker said, sounding disappointed. "His dad teaches high school social studies in Tarrytown, New York. Carl was on the track team at his high school—same town. But he was just, like, on the team. He didn't break any state records, or school records for that matter. A nerd, not an athlete, I guess."

"I'm sure he tried," Diane pointed out.

"Probably just to please his parents," said Parker just as pointedly.

Rose knew Parker and Diane were continually at war over Parker's lackluster grades versus her passion for winterguard and dance, but she didn't want to get into that bit of family drama. "Okay, now go back to Sara. Look her up on Google and see what you can find."

Parker obliged. "Well, her Facebook page, of course. And some art shows her stuff was in. Photos of her artwork. And oh, she teaches at the Wheatfield Alternative High School, and she's a member of the Connecticut Indie Artists. Here's something: she illustrated a children's book, and here's her email address and phone number in case you want to hire her to illustrate something for you."

"Paper," Rose snapped at Diane, who magically produced a grocery pad and pen.

"So are we done?" Parker asked. "I've got to plug in the tablet before I leave for winterguard."

"What about my delicious ziti?" Rose protested.

"Parker will think it's just as delicious at nine o'clock," Diane assured her. "I'll be back to eat with you in a few minutes. Right now I've got to drop Parks off at guard."

And in less than a minute, Parker and Diane had thrown on coats and dashed out the door, leaving Rose with much to think about. She tapped her pen on Diane's grocery pad thoughtfully before writing.

1. Could Betsy's antibiotics make her delusional enough to get lost?
2. What is the real relationship between Carl, Greg and Betsy? How does Sara fit in?
3. Why did Carl tell Betsy there was a serial killer? To get her out of town, but why?
4. If there wasn't a serial killer, who was the man who bought the cake?
5. Why was he wearing silver contact lenses, and why was he dressed so oddly?
6. Who killed the cat and left it behind the bakery? And why?

Right now, Rose didn't have enough information to answer any of those questions. But she planned to keep digging tomorrow, and she hoped Levi's post-mortem on the cat would shed some light in the final question, which really worried Rose. Because someone cruel enough to kill a cat might be cruel enough to kill a person.

When Diane returned, Rose had pulled the ziti out of the oven and was quickly spooning it into bowls.

"I have a really important question to ask you," Rose said. She produced a scrap of paper from her pocket and tossed it across the table to Diane. "That's the kind of antibiotic Betsy was taking. What is it? I know I've had it before."

"You probably have," Diane said. "It's commonly prescribed for urinary tract infections, upper respiratory infections, that sort of thing."

"Could it cause delusions? I mean, could you lose your way or take the wrong bus?"

"Good Lord, no. It wouldn't cause anything worse than maybe a little queasiness or mild diarrhea. Probably not even that. Aren't you going to say grace? I got the idea this is your new thing."

Rose shot her daughter an evil look, crossed herself, and recited the standard Catholic blessing over a meal. Then she grabbed a slice of whole wheat bread and sought to disguise its taste and texture with several tablespoons of butter. "I have a few more questions, so pay attention. We're assuming that Vincent is right and the man in the bakery was wearing silver contact lenses, which he could easily get on the Internet. But Betsy also said he was wearing a fedora and an old-fashioned suit. Why would he have been dressed like that, and where would he get those clothes?"

"I don't know for sure, of course, but I would guess that he wanted to have exactly the effect on Betsy that he did have. The silver contact lenses frightened her so much that she couldn't identify anything else about him. The suit and hat would have seemed so strange, they'd have the same

65

effect. As to the source of the clothes—any vintage clothing shop would have a 1940s fedora, or even the theater department at the university if you didn't want to leave campus."

"So Carl sent this theater major down to the bakery to scare Betsy into leaving town? Why would he do that?"

"Your guess is as good as mine," Diane said. "But it wouldn't have to be a theater major. Anyone with access to the Anderson Center would do."

"The Anderson Center?"

"The theater at Binghamton University. Honestly, Mom, don't you get out at all?"

Rose deliberately ignored that. "I'll have to ask Murray. He seems like a theater sort of person."

"So you and Murray are sleuthing buddies now?"

"He can definitely be useful," Rose admitted. "And he can be charming, which comes in handy. Plus, he's got a good head on his shoulders."

"What did he used to do?" Diane asked. "I mean, before he retired?"

"I wondered that myself," Rose said. "I always saw him in some kind of doddering job—like a guy who repairs clocks—until the other day, when his professional side came out. He mentioned running a furniture store."

"Of course, Zimmerman's! They used to be the go-to place for the high-rent district."

Rose nodded. "I just never made the connection before, and when I did, it really took me by surprise."

"Mama's got a boyfriend, Mama's got a boyfriend," Diane chanted.

"Diana Maria!" Rose scolded. "You know better than that! I would never date anyone who wasn't Roman Catholic!"

"Rosa Helena," Diane said demurely. "I said you were dating. I never said you had to marry him."

Chapter Ten
Friday, February 6
8:00 a.m.

Rose woke up every morning between seven and eight a.m., read the paper over a cup of tea and a slice of toast, and completed her everyday chores—making the bed, picking up the living room, tossing in a load of laundry, maybe a little light dusting or vacuuming. Today she had an extra chore—feeding Daniel—before she worked up the courage to phone Sara Mangero.

"Hello?" The voice on the other end of the phone sounded pleasant, friendly, young.

Rose explained who she was and quickly emphasized that she didn't know if anything had happened to Betsy. "But we haven't seen her in three days, she hasn't been home to feed her cat, and the other neighbors and I are concerned. We thought you might know where she is."

"No, I haven't heard from her in a couple of months. But then my phone has been out for almost a week—I just broke down and bought a new one last night. Same phone number, just different phone. I hope she hasn't been trying to call me, but I kind of doubt she has."

"What would make you say that?" Rose asked.

"Well, we kind of had a falling-out. Over a guy, which is a stupid thing to fight over. She thought the guy liked her more than he did, and I thought she was setting herself up for a big fall. On the other hand, she accused me of just wanting to date him myself. He and I kicked around a bit in high school so I can see why she'd think that, but that wasn't why I was discouraging the relationship. It's—complicated."

"By any chance, was this guy named Greg Thomas?"

"Oh, so you knew about it." Sara sighed. "He just isn't interested in her, and she's absolutely crazy about him. The whole situation is really uncomfortable. Greg and I dated in our senior year of high school, and Betsy practically stalked us. We'd go to the movies—there was Betsy. We'd go to a party, and Betsy would show up. She was trying to convince Greg to take her to the senior prom—she was only a sophomore—but our mother told her she couldn't go. Betsy was furious because Mom was on my side. She snuck out of the house and showed up at the after-prom party anyway."

"Didn't this settle down when you and Greg went to college?" Rose asked.

"Greg and I went to two different colleges so we broke up. I'm an artist—he's a musician—we have different interests. But by that time Betsy had convinced herself that I just didn't want her to have any friends at all. Really, it wasn't that—I wanted to have my own friends, and I wanted her to have hers. She has some developmental issues and can be a bit of a challenge. But then, if you live near her, you probably know."

Rose didn't quite know how to reply. On the one hand, she did know that Betsy could be challenging. On the other hand, she was feeling increasingly sorry for Betsy, who seemed so alone in the world. "When was the last time you saw her?"

Sara sighed again. "My mom died of cancer in August, and Greg came to the funeral. We talked for a long time at the wake, and of course Betsy was right there, practically in our faces. Greg said he was moving to upstate New York because he'd gotten a graduate fellowship at Binghamton University. The next thing I knew, Betsy had quit her job here and she was moving to Binghamton too. She didn't even help clear out my mom's things."

"And you haven't talked to your sister since August?" Rose asked in astonishment. She talked to her own sister, Marie, every weekend.

"Betsy made it abundantly clear that she didn't want to talk to me," Sara said. "She felt this was her big chance to get together with Greg, and she didn't want me to interfere in any way. So I haven't. I haven't spoken to Betsy, and in the past month or so, I haven't spoken to Greg."

"I'm so sorry," Rose said. "It's hard not having family around."

"I miss my mom," Sara said, in a voice suddenly thick with tears. "A lot. But I truthfully don't miss Betsy. I don't want anything bad to have happened to her, of course—I'm not a monster—but I really don't want to have a relationship with her if it's going to be like this. We have a very active arts community here in Litchfield, I have wonderful friends, and I'm very happy here. They're my family now."

"Well, I'm glad we've had a chance to talk," Rose told her. "If I hear anything about Betsy one way or the other, do you want me to call you back?"

"Oh, of course," Sara said. "I wish I could give you more information, or even point you in the direction of somebody who could help you. But I'm sure if you contacted Greg, he'd tell you the same thing."

Rose had no sooner hung up than she heard a knock at the door. At first her heart leapt up in her chest in the hopes that it was Betsy—but this knock was too polite, too restrained. Checking the little fisheye peephole, she found Murray's distorted face peering at her above a purple polka-dot tie and lavender striped shirt. She opened the door.

Murray made a little bow. "I was afraid you might not be up and around so early, but I see you've completed your toilette."

"My toilet is fine," Rose said, wondering why he thought she had a problem with her plumbing. "Isn't yours working? You're welcome to use mine while you wait for the landlord."

She wondered why Murray was chuckling as he poured himself a cup of tea.

"That pink turtleneck looks nice on you, by the way," he commented. "Brings out the color in your cheeks."

Murray's compliment brought out even more, and Rose quickly turned away to refresh her own tea. "I'm glad you came over, because I found out lots of information at Diane's last night. You have no idea how much you can find out about somebody on the computer!"

"I have a little idea," Murray said, "and what little I know is disturbing. But why don't you tell me what you learned?"

Feeling more composed, Rose brought Murray up to speed on Greg, Carl, and Sara, and then added details from her somewhat troubling conversation with Sara that morning.

"Wow," Murray said when she'd finished. "I feel like I should have taken notes. Will there be a quiz on that?"

Rose tossed him the top sheet from Diane's grocery pad. "Last night while Diane was taking Parker to winterguard, I came up with this list of questions about the case."

Murray gazed down at Rose's notes.

"Well," he said, "we know the antibiotics wouldn't make anybody delusional. And we know more about the real relationship between Greg and Betsy than we did yesterday, but I'd like to hear Greg's side of the story."

"Agreed," Rose said. "And we know what Sara says about her own relationship with Greg, but we don't know if that's the truth."

"Question three, why did Carl want Betsy out of town—we still have no answer to that. Let's hold off on question four—who was the man who bought the cake—because I think when we know *why* he bought the cake, question four will answer itself. I really am baffled about the serial killer business."

"There was no serial killer, Murray. It was just a ploy to scare Betsy."

"Yes, but why? Why would you specifically want to scare bakery employees?"

"Employee," Rose corrected. "There was no one there but Betsy."

"Again," Murray said, "why? Normally in the afternoon, there would be at least one other employee there—either the owner Samantha, or Eileen, or in the morning, Justin. But Silver Eyes shows up at a time that he knows Justin will have left, and he knows Samantha will be setting up the trade show, and he knows Eileen went home sick."

"I don't think we can assume that," Rose said. "The only people who would have known the schedule and whereabouts of every employee would have been the other employees. And they obviously weren't Silver Eyes, because Betsy would have recognized them. Take Justin, the baker. Justin dressed up in a suit, wearing silver contact lenses and a fedora, would still look like Justin."

"Okay, so we don't have enough information to answer questions four or five," Murray conceded. "I thought maybe we did. I do have some information about the cat, though."

"Daniel Striped Tiger?"

"No, not Betsy's cat. The cat we found in the dumpster."

Rose had temporarily forgotten that Murray's grandson was going to take a look at it. "So what did Levi find?"

"The cat was not poisoned," Murray said. "It was hit by a speeding car."

"In an alley?" Rose asked skeptically. "That alley can't be more than twelve feet wide, and it's got a dumpster in it. You couldn't drive a car down the alley with that dumpster there, much less a *speeding* car."

"I don't think that's what happened. I think our perpetrator found a dead cat by the side of the road, picked it up, and put it in the alley by the piece of cake. Maybe he knew Betsy had a cat, and wanted her to think this could happen to *her* cat. Maybe he didn't know Betsy had a cat, and he wanted her to think this could happen to her. Either way, he just used what he found by the side of the road, intending it as a sort of message."

"How do you know he didn't kill the cat?"

"Levi's teacher said the cat was dead a good two days before it was placed in the alley," Murray said. "I just think it's unlikely it was killed for that purpose."

"So now," Rose said, "we've still got more investigating to do. What's our next stop?"

Murray smiled. "I think I ought to buy a lovely lady some tickets to the symphony."

Chapter Eleven
Friday, February 6
10:00 a.m.

"Parking garages give me the heebie-jeebies," Rose complained as Murray slowly navigated his Cadillac through the dim structure outside the university theater.

"Why?" Murray asked. He had put a navy wool topcoat over his lavender shirt and red suspenders, and his perky purple bow tie peeped out between the lapels. He looked rather dapper, Rose thought.

"Haven't you ever seen a movie where something awful happened in a parking garage? A mugging. Or a murder."

"I actually don't see very many movies," Murray said, steering into the first available spot. "They depress me."

"What do you do for entertainment?" Rose asked, unbuckling her seat belt and sliding out of the front seat.

"I play the clarinet. I'm surprised you haven't heard me. I also read a lot—history, mostly. And I do like to read mysteries, just not watch them."

"You don't know what you're missing," Rose grumbled, trailing behind him as he ascended a flight of stairs toward the Peace Quad. She hated following people, but she had never been on the Binghamton University campus before and truly had no idea where she was going. Murray, on the other hand, was obviously was no stranger here, and she was grudgingly impressed by his confidence.

They turned right toward a two-story brick building fronted by a low portico.

"I'm not completely sure where the Music Department office is, but it ought to be in this building," Murray remarked, holding a glass door open so Rose could enter.

"I'm sure we could get tickets to the symphony at the Anderson Center box office, but I don't think they'd be as gossipy there. Department offices are notoriously chatty."

Fortunately, just inside the door they spotted a directory on the pale yellow tile wall. It listed the location of the music department office as Room 165. A long hallway leading off to the left looked like a likely site for offices, and sure enough, Room 165 was about halfway down on the left.

The small office was made even smaller by a chest-high counter separating visitors from staff. On the staff side of the counter a pixie-faced girl stood engrossed in a deep conversation with a dark-eyed Asian boy, who leaned toward her on the visitor's side. When Rose and Murray entered, both young people looked up as if startled from a thousand-year sleep.

"Hello, can I help you?" the girl asked. The boy scowled, appearing disgruntled at having his tête-à-tête interrupted.

"I hope so," Murray said. "We want to purchase some tickets for the University Symphony concert next Saturday night—the concert with Greg Thomas—and we went to the Anderson Center box office but no one was there."

"It's a little early," the girl replied. "The box office normally doesn't open until noon."

"Oh dear," Murray said. "That's too bad! Rosie, we've made this whole trip for nothing."

"We can't wait until noon to buy tickets," Rose said in a slight whine. Murray's look said she'd played that to perfection.

"My wife doesn't like to give our credit card number over the phone," Murray said to the girl in a confidential tone. "All that credit card fraud. It's a big problem for us seniors. And we have to be back in town at 11:30."

There was a slight pause. Then the girl said, "I do have some tickets here I could sell you. I'd actually set them aside for my aunt and uncle, but I'm not even sure they'll be in town that night. So why don't you take them—good center seats, row H."

"Oh, we couldn't take their seats!" Murray said.

"Honest, it's okay," the girl said, pressing the tickets into Murray's hand. "If they do come, I'll find them another spot."

Murray handed her cash and passed the tickets over to Rose, who put them in her purse. "Now you'll get to hear your Greg Thomas," he told Rose, who looked appropriately rapturous.

The girl glanced over at her Asian friend before returning her gaze to Rose. "You know," she said conspiratorially, "I bet Greg's here now, down in the practice rooms. They're pretty soundproof, but you might be able to hear him through the door. And if you're lucky, he might pop out and say hello."

"Really?" Rose gasped delightedly, and Murray asked, "How would we get to the practice rooms?"

The girl gave them directions. Murray thanked her, grasped Rose's elbow, and steered her out into the corridor. After a few quick zigs and zags from one hallway into another, he leaned against the wall and dissolved in laughter.

"What did I do?" she asked.

"Absolutely nothing wrong—you were perfect!"

"Then why are you laughing?"

Murray wiped his eyes. "Because, my dear, you fulfilled my every dream. If you could make kugel, I'd marry you!"

"Well, what makes you think I'd marry *you*?" Rose blurted out. She instantly regretted her outburst, but it was true. This was starting to feel like a relationship, and she wasn't sure she wanted a relationship; she certainly could never have a relationship with a Jew, could she? Or could she? Flushing, she sneaked a glance over at Murray and was relieved to see he was still laughing.

"Are you up for one more side trip, possibly with another acting job attached?" he asked.

"Of course," Rose said, pulling herself together. "I'm not decrepit, you know."

They descended a stairway and entered a hallway lined with doors. Although the building was old and utilitarian, the air was alive with a cacophony of orchestral music. Pianos, French horns, flutes, bassoons—but one door resounded with the mournful tones of a cello.

Murray stopped outside the cellist's room and suddenly began to cough loudly. On the third or fourth vigorous cough, he slammed the heel of his hand on the door.

"Murray, what's wrong with you?" Rose asked in genuine alarm. He shook his head and kept coughing. The door opened and Greg Thomas appeared.

He was even more handsome in person than he was in photographs, but Rose could think only of the coughing man beside her.

"Murray! Murray!" She turned to Greg. "Do you have any water in here? Or a place for him to sit down? Murray! Are you having a heart attack?"

Greg helped Murray into the practice room and seated him in a plastic chair. Twisting the top off a fresh bottle of water, he handed it to Rose.

She tipped it up to Murray's lips. "Try and take some of this," she commanded.

"Slowly—slowly—not too fast," Greg advised.

Murray took a sip, then another, and finally wiped the back of his hand across his mouth.

"Wow!" he said. "I don't know what came over me. I was just saying to my wife that I think we're lost, and then suddenly—wait a minute! Aren't you Greg Thomas?"

Greg exposed a mouthful of perfectly straight, perfectly white teeth. "I am."

"We've got tickets to see you in the symphony next Saturday!" Rose gushed.

Greg's smile widened, if that were even possible. "I hope your husband will be well enough to enjoy the concert then."

"Oh, I'm sure I'll be fine," Murray said, thumping his chest with his closed fist. "The ticker's really as sound as a bell."

There was an awkward pause that Rose felt compelled to fill.

"I was so sorry to read about your roommate in the paper," she said. "That was your roommate, wasn't it? The boy who died?"

Greg's smile didn't dim at all, but something in his eyes changed. "Did you know Carl?"

"Not personally, no," Rose said. "But we're neighbors of Betsy Mangero's. She used to talk about you all the time—both of you, actually."

This time the smile lost all semblance of a smile and twisted into something unpleasant. "Carl was very fond of Betsy. She was very fond of me, and that got awkward."

"Between you and Carl?" Rose asked.

"Between me and Betsy. Carl and I were fine."

"Carl's accident must have come as a terrible shock," Murray said.

"Yes, it did. There's no good way to hear something like that."

"I hope you weren't home when it happened," Rose asked. "Because Betsy thought maybe you were."

"I was here." Greg looked at Rose, then Murray, then back at Rose again. "Practicing."

"We're glad to hear you weren't there," Murray said. "Bad enough you have to live through the loss of your friend. It's a mitzvah, your being here with your fellow musicians, who would all be able to comfort you in your time of sorrow."

Greg picked up his bow almost aggressively. "You seem to have recovered, so if you'll excuse me, I need to get back to work. The concert is only a week away."

"Of course," Murray said, standing up and taking Rose's elbow. "We're sorry to have interrupted you. But thank you so much for the water. We'll look forward to hearing you a week from tomorrow."

"I hope you will enjoy it," Greg said formally. There was no beauty in him now; he was carved out of ice.

The door closed behind them, and Rose and Murray once again found themselves in the dim hallway lined with doors.

"Well, that didn't go as well as I might have hoped," Murray said once they'd made their way up a short stairway toward the open air. "You brought up the roommate too soon."

"Well, what did you expect me to talk about? Tchaikovsky?" Rose demanded. "Besides, he's hiding something."

"He most certainly is," Murray agreed. "There's something about that nice young man that isn't nice at all."

During the fifteen-minute ride back to their apartment building, Rose and Murray were uncharacteristically quiet; they still had more questions than answers. Murray pulled his ancient Cadillac into its accustomed spot, and Rose waited while he draped it with the ripstop nylon cover that protected its flawless paint job. As they came around the front of the building, Vincent's car pulled up and parked at the curb.

He didn't look happy. "We need to talk," he said to Rose.

"So come upstairs," she told him. They trudged up the stairs to the second floor. Murray stopped in front of his own door and pulled out his key.

"Uh-uh, Dr. Watson," Vincent said to Murray. "You too."

He pointed toward Rose's apartment. She unlocked the door and everyone went in.

"What is this, Vincent?" Rose asked, sitting down on the loveseat. "I feel like I'm about to get the third degree."

"We found Betsy." Vincent leaned back against the closed door. "In a mom and pop motel in Newburgh, New York. She checked in Wednesday night."

"That was the night she was supposed to come to dinner!" Rose said. "What on earth is she doing in Newburgh? Why didn't she call? Is she all right?"

"No," Vincent said. "She isn't. She's dead."

Chapter Twelve
Friday, February 6
12:30 p.m.

"Vincent, Betsy can't be dead," Rose said, her throat tight. "She simply can't be."

"Unofficially, it's Betsy—I've seen the photos—but officially we don't have a positive identification yet, because we haven't located next of kin—"

"It's Sara Mangero," Murray told him gravely. "A sister. She's an artist in Litchfield, Connecticut. Their mother is dead so she's probably next of kin."

"I have her number," Rose added. She copied it from her grocery pad onto a fresh sheet of paper and handed it to Vincent.

"Thanks," Vincent said. "That'll help. But that sort of thing is the reason I want to talk to you two. Do you realize that in New York State, you can't become a private investigator without a license?"

"What do you mean?" Rose sputtered.

"Let's put it this way," Vincent said. "I call the Cakery on Court Street to interview the workers, and they tell me you've been there and talked to them. I call the university to interview the roommate of the Feinstein kid, and he tells me you've just been there and talked to him. If you'd just let the police handle this from the get-go, Betsy might still be alive."

"No, no, no." Rose shot up off the loveseat. "You are not going to dump that on me, Vincent Bevelacqua. On Monday a weird guy came into the shop where Betsy worked, bought a cake, and left a slice of it on our front doorstep. I called you. You said you can't 'use her' because she's a fruit loop.

On Tuesday Betsy witnessed a suspicious death. I called you. You told me she still wasn't 'credible'—"

"Why?" Murray interrupted.

"She's a fruit loop, remember?" She turned back to Vincent. "And you told her not to leave town, like she was a suspect instead of a victim. On Wednesday, I invited her to dinner and she didn't show up. I called you. And you seemed more upset about the Feinsteins hiring a lawyer to prevent an autopsy than you were about Betsy – you said she probably had a better offer or got lucky. Now, you knew Betsy. Did she strike you as the sort of person who would tend to get lucky?"

"No, but—" Vincent began.

"But nothing. You'd given up on her. The next day, Wednesday, she still wasn't home. I had to go into her apartment and get her cat, who was yowling and screeching and putting up a terrible fuss—"

"Did you have a key?"

"Am I finished? Do I *sound* finished? I brought the cat over here because I figured that something had happened to Betsy and there's no reason the cat should starve. Murray and I went down to the bakery where she worked to find out if they knew where she had gone. The one employee we spoke with didn't know anything."

"Bupkus," Murray affirmed.

"Now, if you call that 'interviewing,' so be it," Rose went on. "I call it loving your neighbor—something you don't seem to be good at, by the way. This worker, Eileen, told us that a dead cat was left in the alley right outside the back door of the shop. The cat was curled up around a takeout box of chocolate cake crumbs. If Betsy had been the first person to find it, that would have upset her plenty. Upset enough to take off for Newburgh? I don't know, because she didn't call me. But if she had, I sure as hell would not have called you."

"Did it ever dawn on you that the cat might have been poisoned?" Vincent asked.

"Of course," Murray said. "My grandson Levi did a post-mortem. The cat was hit by a car."

Vincent opened his mouth but Rose's glare shut him up.

"It's still my turn," Rose said. "So next we wanted to find out the real relationship between Betsy, Greg, and Carl. I called Betsy's sister Sara—Parker got her number off the computer. Sara told me that she'd dated Greg in high school and Betsy was jealous, to the point of stalking them when they were out together. When Betsy found out Greg was going to Binghamton University, she moved here, probably with the intent of stalking him again. There's plenty more we could tell you, but it's your turn. Tit for tat. You sit down and tell us what you know."

Vincent shook his head. "Ma, that's not how it works. I ask the questions."

"Well, then I guess you're not too interested in hearing our answers, are you?" She turned to Murray. "I have some lovely onion bagels I put in the freezer. Would you like one?"

"Toasted?" Murray said. "I like mine toasted. Just shy of burnt. With cream cheese, if you have any."

"I could arrange that." Rose turned toward the kitchen.

"Ma," Vincent said. "Come back. Sit down. I'll tell you as much as I can."

She looked at Murray, who confirmed that his bagel could wait for a minute.

The three sat down around the coffee table.

"We got a call from the police in Newburgh about nine this morning," Vincent said. "The cleaning staff at the motel found Betsy dead in her room. The Newburgh police think she's been dead about twenty-four hours, but there will be an autopsy to confirm that. She was wearing normal daytime clothes—a polo shirt with 'The Cakery' embroidered on it, black pants, sneakers. The desk clerk said those were the clothes she wore when she registered for the room three days ago. There's no evidence that the body was moved; there seems to have been a bit of a scuffle that ended with Betsy getting stabbed with a long knife of some sort—"

"A cake knife?" Murray asked with narrowed eyes.

"Too soon to make that determination. It could have been. It could also have been a thousand other implements."

"Did they find her phone?"

"Her phone?" Vincent consulted his notes. "She didn't have a phone on her, no. And no luggage of any kind, which seems strange since she'd stayed in the motel for two days."

"She had to have her phone!" Rose said. "She never went anywhere without it! Do you think that the guy Carl tried to warn her about killed Betsy and stole her phone?"

"Ma, the guy Carl tried to warn her about doesn't exist. If we didn't have two dead bodies on our hands, I'd assume Carl's serial killer was a practical joke."

"But you do have two dead bodies on your hands," Murray pointed out. "So something has to be going on. What's the story with Carl's parents and the autopsy?"

Vincent sighed in exasperation. "Betsy insisted Carl was pushed, but as I told my mother, Betsy wasn't a credible witness. Fortunately, the crime scene investigators are inclined to agree with Betsy's statement—Carl seems to have been pushed, and he tried to break his fall by grabbing at the curtains, pulling the curtain bracket away from the wall. Because Carl's death was both unattended and suspicious, we ordered an autopsy. The day after Carl's death, his parents came up from Florida where they're spending the winter. Their home is in Westchester County—Tarrytown, I think they said. Anyway, they wanted Carl buried immediately, that same day, without an autopsy."

"Well, sure. They're Orthodox," Murray said.

"Doesn't matter. There has to be an autopsy. We got a judge to rule in our favor and the autopsy went forward. We were really looking for drugs—something that would cause a person standing near the window to lose his balance and tumble out—or further evidence that he was forcibly pushed. We didn't find the drugs."

"So he was pushed out the window?" Rose asked.

"From the position of the body upon landing and the way the glass broke and scattered in the street, it seems likely, yes. At least I would say there was some kind of struggle right near the window, which ended with an outward thrust."

"Did you release Carl's body to the Feinsteins?" Murray pulled a tiny address book from his breast pocket. "I can give you the number of a local Hevra Kadisha—the Jewish burial society. They can help the family ensure everything is done properly."

"But why the rush?" Rose asked.

"If they're Orthodox, they would want the body washed and wrapped in a shroud, but not embalmed," Murray said. "They put the body in a plain wooden box—not airtight, not lined—and the body should be in the ground, intact and unmutilated, within twenty-four hours of death. Conservative and Reform Jews are a little less strict in their rules, but most observant Jews try to keep as close to that standard as they can."

"So what else have you found out?" Rose asked Vincent.

"Not as much as you have," he admitted. "I was really focused on securing Carl's autopsy and getting the results. It wasn't until this morning, after I got the call from Newburgh, that I tried contacting anyone at BU or the cake shop. I still don't really know where I'm going with either case. There doesn't seem to be anything connecting Carl's fall in Binghamton with Betsy's assault in Newburgh except the fact that they knew one another."

"Does that mean Greg's not safe either?" Rose asked. "Or Sara?"

"Or is one of them the murderer?" Murray countered.

Vincent held up his index finger. "Now comes the cautionary part. I get why you felt the need to investigate Betsy's disappearance in light of my—disinterest, let us say."

Rose huffed and sat back.

"But this is a police investigation now," Vincent went on. "There have been two suspicious deaths. I want you both to back off."

Murray opened his mouth, and Vincent waggled his upraised finger—a mannerism picked up from his mom.

"This is not a request. It is an order. Get a new hobby. Learn mah jongg. Take up line dancing. But stop investigating these crimes. The police can handle this perfectly well—that's why we're here."

Rose and Murray looked at each other.

"All right," Rose said at last. "I know you just want me to be safe."

"Exactly," Vincent said, snapping his notebook shut and standing up. "Now, I have to go. Remember your promise."

"I remember," Rose said in her most docile voice.

After the door closed behind Vincent, Murray asked Rose, "Were you crossing your fingers?"

"I was," Rose said. "But there's one more thing I need to do. I need to call Sara. Because I made that promise first—and my fingers weren't crossed then."

* * *

Sara cried when Rose told her, and Rose cried too. Sara's pain seemed all the more terrible given how estranged she'd felt from Betsy only a few days before. Rose understood that too; she'd felt estranged from Anthony before he came home, terminally ill, and asked her to take him in. She'd been able to reconcile with Anthony before he died; Sara hadn't had that chance. Rose assured Sara that Vincent would take over the case and he would give it the highest priority.

"But you're going to keep looking for her killer, aren't you?" Sara cried. "You're not going to give up?"

"I have to, Sara," Rose told her. "It's an active police investigation now. I can't interfere."

"You don't have to interfere," Sara said. "Just keep asking questions. Just keep looking. I think most people would be much more willing to talk to you than they would the police. Please don't give up on my sister!"

And Rose promised she wouldn't, knowing that was in complete contrast to what she'd just promised Vincent. But there had to be justice for Betsy, and she had to be the one to find it.

Chapter Thirteen
Saturday, February 7
7 a.m.

Rose only slept for an hour or two Friday night. Her head swam. Whoever killed Betsy wasn't a stranger—it was someone who was part of her life. Rose mentally scrolled through the list. Her estranged sister Sara, whose feelings for Betsy had changed dramatically since her death. The guy Betsy loved, Greg, who didn't love her. The baker, Justin, who used to room with Carl. Betsy's co-worker, Eileen, who encouraged the boss to fire her. Betsy's boss, Samantha, who was still an unknown quantity. Was there anyone else? There may have been—but if so, Rose didn't know who they were.

She made herself a cup of tea, cracked open a steno pad she had purchased for church council notes, and started to organize her thoughts.

Sara Mangero
- Motive: Unknown, but may have some ongoing feeling for Greg, or an ongoing involvement
- Opportunity: Could she have been in Newburgh on Thursday? How to find out?
- Means: Would she be strong enough to overpower Betsy and stab her? Artists know anatomy; is that relevant?

Greg Thomas
- Motive: Betsy was stalking him, and despite a police warning, she didn't stop doing it. Is that a serious enough reason to kill someone?

- Opportunity: To kill Betsy, Greg would have to have been in Newburgh on Thursday. Was he?
- Means: Definitely strong enough.

Justin Hopko
- Motive: Unknown.
- Opportunity: Rose and Murray saw him at work in Binghamton on Thursday morning, but if Betsy was killed early Thursday afternoon, he would have had time to get to Newburgh.
- Means: Like Greg, strong enough.

Eileen Reeves
- Motive: Unknown; she seems to have considered Betsy incompetent and annoying, but that's no reason to kill her.
- Opportunity: Unlikely; Eileen was manning the Cakery alone Thursday morning and she seemed to have been stuck there, so she couldn't be in Newburgh
- Means: Not much power in those skinny arms.

Samantha Truesdell
- Motive: Unknown.
- Opportunity: Eileen said Samantha was at a Chamber of Commerce trade show on Thursday morning, which would be easy enough to check.
- Means: Unknown.

Another question: Who else could be considered a suspect?

Yet another question: Was there a connection between Carl's deaths and Betsy's?

Still another question: Who was the "serial killer" who bought the cake?

Rose nibbled her pen in frustration. Too many unknowns. And for every detail that would be easy to check—like whether Samantha was really at the trade show—there were questions that would be much harder to answer, such motive or means.

For this, she'd need help.

She picked up the phone and dialed Murray's number, knowing that he was an early riser, too. After five rings, the answering machine came on, telling her to leave a message after the beep.

"Murray?" she asked rhetorically. "It's Rose. We need to get together and come up with a plan. Call me."

He didn't phone right back, so Rose took a shower, dried her hair, and dressed. She tried Murray's number again, then she made the bed and ran the vacuum. After the third attempt to call Murray, she washed the breakfast dishes and cleaned out the refrigerator. Finally she glanced at the clock. It was 11:30. Where in the world could Murray be? She waited another hour, picked up her steno pad, stormed across the hall and pounded on his door.

"Come in," Murray called pleasantly.

Rose opened the door into a living room that looked more like a library than a residential space. Bookshelves lined every wall, and wooden slatted blinds filtered the winter light. Murray sat in a comfortable recliner beneath the glow of a 1930s gooseneck floor lamp. He was wearing a worn velvet yarmulke.

"Good morning, Rosie," Murray said. "Have a seat."

"Is there something wrong with your telephone?" Rose demanded.

"Not that I know of."

"I've been calling you for hours!"

"I'm one of those old-fashioned Jews who doesn't answer the phone on Shabbat." Seeing Rose's look of confusion, he translated. "The Sabbath. Catholics don't eat meat on Fridays during Lent; I don't answer the phone on Shabbat."

"This is Shabbat right now?" asked Rose.

"It is. Your Sabbath is on Sunday. Ours starts on Friday night and runs until Saturday evening."

Rose pulled up a chair and opened her steno pad. "Well, let me show you what I've been doing. I've charted out all the people in Betsy's life, and who has motive, means, and opportunity to commit the crime—"

"Stop there," Murray said. "I don't solve crimes on Shabbat."

"Excuse me?"

"I've enjoyed helping you try to find whoever is responsible for Greg and Betsy's deaths. Plus, I think we are making a valuable contribution toward the solution of the crime, though I know your son doesn't agree. But on Shabbat that would be work, so it would be forbidden. You'll have to wait till tomorrow."

"That is the dumbest thing I ever heard!" Rose said. "Your brain doesn't turn off on the Sabbath, does it?"

"Of course not, but it turns to higher things."

Rose peered over to see what he was reading; it was *The Book of Joy*, by the Dalai Lama.

"I focus on things that will engage my spirit and expand my mind," Murray explained, "and turn off the hubbub of the modern world. I don't expect you to understand."

"That's good, because I don't. What would you do if somebody was dying on the hearthrug?"

"I would call 911, definitely," Murray said. "But as you can see, no one is dying on the hearthrug. The two people who have already died are beyond my immediate assistance. Now, if you don't mind, I'd like to get back to my reading. Keeping Shabbat restores my spirit, and I really need it after the week we've had. But perhaps waiting until tomorrow does cost us valuable time. Can we meet and discuss your notes tonight, after Shabbat is over? 7:30, perhaps?"

"You could come over for dinner," Rose said. "How about vegetarian chili? With a nice green salad, and cornbread."

"That would be great." Murray looked down at his book and chuckled.

"What's so funny?"

He waved a hand dismissively. "It's nothing. Something my son David said last night at dinner."

"What did he say?"

"We can talk about it later," Murray said, picking up his book again. "Not now."

Rose returned to her apartment, frustrated.

It was the longest Saturday ever. She walked to Price Chopper, picking up the ingredients for her chili and cornbread dinner. It wasn't an expensive dinner but it was a bulky one, and she wished she'd thought to bring her folding shopping cart. She felt like a bag lady sweating in her heavy coat, hauling her ugly polypropylene totes down the street.

At home, she chopped an onion, a green pepper, and some garlic. She put the vegetables she'd just chopped together with canned beans, tomatoes, and chili mix into her crockpot and flipped the temperature to low. About an hour before Murray was scheduled to arrive, she mixed the dry yellow cake mix into corn bread mix and beat in the liquid ingredients, eventually pouring the whole thing into a brownie pan. While the cake baked, she grated carrots and radishes and gave them a whirl with the washed lettuce in her salad spinner.

Just after she removed the cornbread from the oven, she heard Murray at the door. "One second!" she called, stripping off her apron and stuffing it behind a couch cushion.

Murray looked spiffy in yet another of his seemingly-endless collection of bow ties. He sniffed appreciatively as he came in and Rose wasted no time in serving him a big bowl of chili with salad and hot cornbread on the side.

"I didn't think you'd be able to surpass your macaroni and cheese. But your chili and cornbread are amazing."

"You don't get out much," Rose said modestly. "They all started with packaged mixes."

"But they didn't end there, and that's the trick," Murray said. "Now—down to business. Where are your notes?"

Rose produced her steno pad. "Here are the five people I have for suspects—Betsy's co-workers, her sister, and Greg. Should I add in the Feinsteins?"

"Carl's parents?" Murray asked, shocked. "Why would they kill their own son?"

"You weren't even a tiny bit disturbed when I suggested that we should consider Betsy's sister," Rose pointed out. "But as to the Feinsteins—I'm just curious about them. Betsy told us the man who bought the cake had dark skin and wore a light grey suit. Where would a light grey suit be even slightly appropriate in February? And where is a common place to get a deep tan? I'll give you a hint—it's where the Feinsteins had been spending the winter."

"Florida? But they didn't come up until Tuesday, after Vincent called them."

"Are you so sure about that?" Rose asked. "You and I are not spring chickens—

"Speak for yourself!" Murray said.

"—and because we grew up in a different world, we always assume that if you phone people who live in Florida, you're speaking to them in Florida. With cell phones, that's not necessarily so. How do we know they weren't already in Binghamton when Vincent phoned them?"

"We don't," Murray admitted, "but I'm not sure there's any way for us to find out. I don't think regular citizens can access other people's phone records. And anyway, what would their motive be?"

"I'm not saying there is one. I'm just saying the Feinsteins might be another avenue to explore."

"Unfortunately, though, by now they're probably back in Tarrytown sitting shiva," Murray pointed out. "So we've missed our window of opportunity."

"Sitting what?"

"Shiva," Murray told her, reaching for the bread basket. "This is really terrific cornbread, Rosie. So light and fluffy! Anyway, shiva is the week-long mourning period after a death. You stay home and welcome visitors who have come to grieve with you. It would be totally inappropriate to barge in and start questioning the family."

"It would be totally inappropriate to kill your son," Rose observed. "So how do we fix this?"

"We wait until they're done sitting shiva. Some families don't sit shiva for a whole week these days—they need to get back to work. I'll make a few calls, pretend I knew Carl, and find out if the Feinsteins plan to cut their shiva short. With any luck I'll learn when they expect to come back to collect Carl's things from his apartment, and we can talk to them then."

Rose tapped her pencil on the pad. "In the meantime, do you think that maybe we've been asking the wrong people? We asked Greg and Sara about Betsy and they told us about themselves. On Monday, let's retrace our steps and ask Sara about Greg and Greg about Eileen and Eileen about Justin and Justin about Samantha—you get the idea."

"Yes, but can I ask why?"

"Simple," Rose said. "Everybody lies. I crossed my fingers when I promised Vincent to stop investigating, but I did it because I think that, knowing Betsy, I can do as good a job of solving her murder as the police can. You're planning to lie to the Feinsteins about knowing Carl, but you're doing it to bring the murderer to justice. In other words, we have a motive for lying. Generally when a person talks about himself, he lies to make himself look more impressive, or in this case, more innocent. When he talks about other people, he's more inclined to tell the truth—unless he has a good reason not to. Those good reasons may solve our mystery."

"You have a very cynical outlook on life," Murray said with a smile.

"Cynical, yes. But it works."

Chapter Fourteen
Sunday, February 8
8:50 a.m.

Every Sunday morning just before nine, Rose could always be found in the sixth pew from the back at St. Casimir Church on Prospect Street. Most Sundays, Diane and Parker would join her there, unless they'd been at a winterguard show the previous night and claimed they were too tired to drag themselves out of bed. Once in a while, Vincent would join them at Mass as well; due to his job, Rose was willing to cut him a little more slack on missing his Sunday obligation than she did the girls. Today, however, she was actually hoping Vincent didn't come. She really didn't want him to find out she was continuing her quest to find Betsy's killer.

She made the sign of the cross and was just about to rise off the kneeler into her pew when Diane and Parker slipped in beside her. Skipping the preliminary prayer, they crossed themselves and sat down.

"How's the sleuthing business?" Diane whispered.

"Took a day off yesterday," Rose answered. "Murray doesn't do anything on the Sabbath. I mean *anything*."

"Wow, that must have come as a shock," Diane said. "Finding someone more pious than you."

"If you start going out with him," Parker teased, "would you take off the whole weekend?"

"I am not going to go out with him," Rose said flatly, staring straight ahead at the magnificent altarpiece. "He's—he's—"

"He's what?" Diane asked. "Smart? Kind? Funny? Interesting?"

"Jewish," said her mother, standing up as the Mass began.

Rose kept her eyes on the priest, chanting the responses as dutifully as a nun, and she avoided looking at either Diane or Parker. She sensed their amusement, and assumed that if she ignored them, they'd stop giggling. Finally, when the introductory rites were over and the lector was mounting the steps for the Old Testament reading, everyone sat down and Rose took the opportunity to glower at her daughter and granddaughter. Unfortunately, this only made them giggle more fiercely.

"At the peace," Rose said under her breath, "you both can go sit on the other side of the church."

"Why can't we go there now?" Diane murmured back. "People over there don't glare at us."

"I wouldn't be glaring—"

An ancient parishioner in a veiled pillbox hat turned around to give Rose a warning glance.

Rose lowered her voice to the barest whisper. "I wouldn't be glaring if you two were acting respectably."

"That lady in the hat didn't give *us* the stink eye," Parker said. "She was looking at you, Nonni."

And then Diane and Parker giggled again. It was hopeless. At the peace—when she should have been wishing nearby worshippers the peace of Christ—Rose spotted her neighbors, the Espositos, sitting a few pews ahead on the other side of the aisle. Mrs. Esposito waved sociably and Rose picked up her clutch purse and abandoned her family to sit with them. She pointedly ignored Diane and Parker when everyone processed forward for communion, and returned to the Espositos' pew until dismissal.

As soon as the last notes of the final song sounded, Mrs. Esposito laid a hand on Rose's arm. "That girl, I hear she die."

Betsy. Rose nodded. "We still don't know what happened."

Mrs. Esposito hiked one eyebrow. "She die in motel, no?"

"I don't think she was there to meet a man."

"She was there to meet woman?" Mrs. Esposito gasped, crossing herself.

Making her way through the throng of people, Rose suddenly felt stupid. If Diane had gone to a town three hours away to meet someone in a motel, Rose would have had no doubt what she planned to do there. But that possibility had never occurred to her in Betsy's case, because Betsy was overweight and homely and wore bad clothes. Maybe the question shouldn't be "What on earth was Betsy doing in Newburgh," but rather, "Who was Betsy in Newburgh to meet?"

"Mom?"

Deep in thought, Rose barely heard her daughter's approach.

"I'm sorry, Mom. Parker and I were being childish."

"Yes, you were. And irreverent. But I don't want to talk about that now."

"Nonni, come on," Parker pleaded. "We're sorry. Really. Let's go out for breakfast and make up."

Rose gave Parker a swift kiss. "Not today. And it's not because I'm mad at you. I was, but I'm over that. I'd appreciate a ride home, though. I need to run something by Murray."

Diane and Parker looked at each other. Neither said a thing.

*   *   *

Murray put his newspaper down. "You want to go where?"

"The bus station," Rose said. "It would be better if we went on Wednesday, because Betsy probably left on a Wednesday and we'd be more likely to talk to the same person who sold Betsy her ticket. But I'm impatient, and I want to test out my theory. So can we go now?"

"How do you know she went to Newburgh on a bus?"

"Because she didn't drive. And I can't think of anyone who would drive her there."

"I can't think of any reason she'd go to Newburgh in the first place," Murray said.

"Well, that's what I want to find out," Rose insisted. "Come on. It's not the Sabbath—for you, anyway—and we can't go down to the University offices because they're closed. Please?"

"Anything for you," Murray said, folding his paper and rising stiffly out of his chair. "Arthritis," he explained unnecessarily. "It's going to rain. I know, I know—another reason we should go to the bus station today and not wait until Monday."

"Exactly," Rose said with satisfaction.

It took Murray five minutes to find a cap that matched his bow tie and a jacket that complemented them both. Then Murray and Rose made their way around the building to the carport where he kept his vintage Cadillac. Murray removed the car's nylon cover, carefully folded it up, crossed to the passenger side, unlocked the car, and gallantly assisted Rose into the front seat before crossing back to the driver's side and getting in himself. Then he backed the Cadillac out of its parking spot and started down Main Street at a snail's pace. Last week Rose would have been itching to wrestle the wheel away from him, but today for some reason he made a warm place in her heart.

At last they swerved onto Chenango Street and pulled to a stop opposite the bus terminal. Rose hopped out of the car and, without waiting for Murray, trotted through the front door and crossed the waiting room to the ticket window. A stocky middle-aged woman whose nametag read *Letitia* asked if she could help.

"I hope so," Rose said. "Did you work this past Wednesday?"

Letitia looked suspicious. "Why?"

"My neighbor bought a bus ticket to Newburgh on Wednesday," Rose said.

"What time? 11:20 or 4:40?"

Rose looked at Murray, who shrugged. "I have no idea," she said.

"What does she look like?"

"About twenty, dark hair, a little on the chubby side. Not glamorous, if you know what I mean—dark pants and a polo shirt, red fleece jacket. Black sneakers. She was probably carrying a Hello Kitty purse."

Letitia had looked totally blank until Rose mentioned the purse. Suddenly her expression brightened. "I do remember her! She came in here about quarter after eleven, all in a rush, and she had no idea where she was going."

"She hadn't planned to go to Newburgh?"

"Nope. She didn't know where she wanted to go, she just wanted to get on a bus right then. Any bus. Going any place."

"That's a little odd, isn't it?"

Letitia laughed. "Honey, everything in this place is odd. You have no idea."

"So you said that the next bus went to Newburgh—"

"No, I didn't. There was a bus just pulling in, and I said it went to Poughkeepsie, but stopped in Monticello, Middletown, Newburgh, and Fishkill first. She seemed to like that idea and said she wanted to go to Newburgh. I told her most people get off at Monticello and transfer to New York City, but she said nope—Newburgh was where she wanted to go."

Murray joined Rose at the counter and smiled engagingly at Letitia. "Hello. I'm with her."

"So what happened then?" Rose asked.

Letitia looked suspicious. "Why do you want to know? Is she in trouble?"

Murray smiled disarmingly. "Oh, no, no—nothing like that. She's our neighbor. We're trying to get in touch with her so we'll know how long we need to take care of her cat."

Letitia visibly relaxed. "Well, if that's all. She paid for her ticket, of course—cash, straight out of a bank envelope. Citizens Bank—I recognized the envelope, because that's where my account is too."

"A lot of cash? A little cash?" asked Rose.

Letitia shrugged. "Not wads and wads, like a drug deal, but maybe ten bills."

Rose looked at Murray. "She cashed her paycheck, I'll bet."

Murray shook his head. "It was what, the fifth of the month? She might have cashed her paycheck to pay the rent."

"So she took out what was left of it," Rose concluded.

"Which means," Murray said to Rose, "on the first of the month she didn't have any plans to leave, but on the fifth of the month she didn't plan to come back."

"Say," Letitia said. "On the radio I heard about some local woman who got stabbed in a motel in Newburgh. You don't think that could be your neighbor, do you?"

Rose's gasp was completely sincere, and Murray stepped in to fill the dead air. "It's terrible, the things that happen these days," he said. "I don't remember hearing such things when I was young. Now it seems to happen every day."

"You sure you're not detectives?" Letitia asked. "I mean, you don't *look* like detectives."

Murray leaned close and spoke very quietly. "The best ones never do."

Rose swatted him on the arm as soon as they were out of earshot. "The best ones never do," she scoffed. "What movie did you get that from?"

Murray hiked his eyebrows knowingly. "One that didn't depress me."

"Well, now we know that Betsy's made the news. That depresses *me*."

Exiting the building, they crossed the street to the Cadillac, and again Murray got Rose comfortably seated on her side of the car before getting in himself. He adjusted his cap and his bow tie in the rearview mirror, placed his hands at ten and two, and looked over at his passenger.

"Next stop?"

Rose considered. "You said you could find out when the Feinsteins will stop shivering."

"Sitting shiva."

"Whatever. How would you do that?"

"A phone call. Maybe two. From the comfort of my living room."

"Then let's go home."

As soon as they pulled into the carport, Rose bounded out of the car and virtually flew up the stairs to Murray's apartment door. He followed at a considerable distance, then took another half minute to isolate a red-capped key from the others on his ring and insert it into the lock. As the door swung open, Rose rushed inside, but Murray took a moment to touch the mezuzah on his doorpost and kiss his fingertips before dropping his keys into the small dish by his door.

"That way I won't have to look for them again," he explained. "A moment of care now prevents ten minutes of panic the next time I go out."

"Whatever," Rose said. "How are you going to find out when the Feinsteins are done with their sitting?"

"Easy," Murray said. "You know I'm from Brooklyn, and I still have lots of friends downstate. My friend Sol lives in Tarrytown, as it happens. Go make yourself a tea—Sol's a talker, so I'm sure I'll be a minute."

Rose ran tap water into two cups and microwaved them while she hunted for teabags, finding a box of Lipton just about the same time that the bell on the microwave announced that the water was hot. She dropped the teabags into both cups, pressed each one against the walls of the cup several times until the tea was the color she liked, and came back into the living room just as Murray was getting well into his conversation. He looked a little guilty when he saw Rose.

"Solly, I'm going to have to call you back—I just have a quick question now. You've got the local paper?"

Sol apparently affirmed that he did.

"Go to the obituaries and look for a Carl Feinstein—oh, you heard about it then," Murray said. "Yes, he fell out of a window, although how that happened nobody knows. —

Found it? Does it say anything about shiva? Through Wednesday." He winked at Rose. "That's too bad. My friend wanted to drive down on Thursday—I know, people don't sit shiva as long as they did in our day. A shame, I agree. Thanks, Sol—you're a mensch."

Murray set the receiver lightly in its cradle and spread his hands. "Ta-da. The Feinsteins are sitting shiva through Wednesday, then they plan to come back up to Binghamton to clean out Carl's apartment."

"And I know two detectives who want to talk to them when they do," said Rose.

Chapter Fifteen
Monday, February 9
9:00 a.m.

Monday morning found Rose knocking on Murray's apartment door. While she waited for him to answer, her gaze wandered to the little cigar-shaped object screwed to his doorpost. It was made of silver and featured a narrow gold tree with a Hebrew letter at the top. She'd seen Murray touch it on his way in and out, and she was mildly curious about its significance. But right now she was much more curious about the deaths of Betsy and Carl.

On the one hand, it was entirely possible that Carl had just fallen out the window backwards, and Betsy had completely imagined the idea that he had been pushed. And it was entirely possible that Betsy had been killed during a random botched burglary attempt in a Newburgh motel, and it had nothing whatsoever to do with Carl's death back in Binghamton. Those were the simplest explanations, and the simplest explanations were usually true—but in this case, Rose didn't believe either one of them.

The door swung open, and there stood Murray, smiling, as dapper and smart as usual. A dove gray silk bow-tie peeked between the lapels of his beautifully-tailored navy topcoat, and he wore a charcoal cap on his head.

"All ready," he announced. "You want to hit the bakery first?"

"Sounds good to me," Rose said, looking him up and down appreciatively. He really was a nice-looking man—not as tall and handsome as her Dom had been, of course, but then she'd fallen in love with Dom when he was twenty-six and she'd aged right alongside him. She didn't know how handsome she would have considered Dom if she'd met him in his eighties. But regardless, she enjoyed walking on the arm of a nicely-dressed man right now, and she was glad she'd worn her favorite raspberry jacket, with the trapunto collar she'd labored over for days.

Once downstairs, they circled the building to the carport and Murray opened the passenger's side door. Rose ran her fingers along the leather seat as if she'd never ridden in the car before. Murray got in the driver's side and she was aware for the first time of his delicious aftershave. The car purred like a contented cat as he backed it into the street.

What in the world was happening to her? She was seventy-four years old! Murray must be close to eighty-five! And he was Jewish! She remembered how upset her family had been when her cousin Marie married a man who was Russian Orthodox. And Russian Orthodox people were still Catholic; they just celebrated Christmas on the wrong day. What would her parents think if they knew she was keeping company with a Jew?

She suddenly realized they were crossing the bridge onto Court Street, and she had missed the beginning of Murray's story.

"—So I called Sol back later last night when we really had time to talk. Turns out he'd known the Feinsteins for years—they actually live in his neighborhood. Carl's father, Ira, is a social studies teacher. Ira also tutors kids for their bar or bat mitzvahs."

"Their what?" Rose asked.

"It's a coming of age ceremony for Jewish children, right around the age of puberty," Murray explained. "As part of the ceremony, they need to read a scripture in Hebrew, and Ira teaches it to them, as well as other things they'll need to know as they grow up in the Jewish faith."

"So you're saying Carl's father is well-educated and very religious."

"That's it in a nutshell, yes. Apparently Carl inherited his father's intelligence. His faith, not so much. He was smart enough to find a thousand ways to do what his parents didn't want him to do."

"My Anthony," Rose said, and then wished she could take the words back; Anthony hadn't been a bad boy, or a bad young man. She just hadn't understood his lifestyle. "What kind of trouble did Carl get into, exactly?"

Murray swerved the Cadillac into a parking spot on Chenango Street. "I hope you don't mind a bit of a walk, but there are never any convenient places to park since the mayor tore the parking garage down."

"He had to. It was *falling* down," Rose pointed out. "You can't preserve everything. Now, you were saying—trouble? Carl?"

"I hadn't forgotten. When Carl was younger—twelve or fourteen—he would steal anything that wasn't nailed down. Then he discovered how to sell things other people stole. He was very lucky his uncle was a lawyer. Then suddenly, in high school, he seemed to straighten up. His grades went from so-so to fantastic. He went to community college and from there he applied to Binghamton and got in as a transfer student. Ira was worried that as soon as Carl got away from home the trouble would all start up again, but apparently it didn't. He did fine in undergraduate school and got a teaching fellowship. The Feinsteins were thrilled, naturally, but there was always that sense that any time the other shoe was going to drop."

"And did it?" Rose asked.

Murray shrugged. "He wound up dead. You tell me."

107

They walked side by side down Court Street, and Rose remembered many years before walking these same pavements with Dom, looking in the windows at Sisson's and David's and Drazen's, buying a bag of nuts at Mr. Peanut or some candy at Fanny Farmer. She would have looped her arm into the crook of Dom's as they walked, and it seemed awkward not to walk that way with Murray—but Murray was not Dom. She was definitely getting Alzheimer's, she decided, and darted ahead of Murray to open the bakery door herself.

The Cakery was even busier than it had been the previous week, with students and state workers and passers-by standing on line, waiting for their purchases to be prepared or sliced or boxed, or seated at the half-dozen bistro tables that dotted the shop floor. A pair of students vacated their table, so Rose grabbed it and Murray got on line to order. While she waited, Rose picked out Eileen and another woman—this must be Samantha, the owner—bustling behind the counter, and she spotted Justin working just as busily in the back.

Samantha was tall and lean, with blonde highlights and the kind of musculature that came from daily stints at the gym. But there was more to it than that. While Eileen gave the impression of a woman wealthy enough to be artsy, Samantha seemed harder somehow, like her graceful acrylics covered nails worked to the bone. The lines of her face were etched sharp with ambition. This was a tireless worker, a woman who wouldn't let something as insignificant as the death of an employee stand in the way of a prosperous Monday morning.

Murray returned with two cups of tea and a huge Morning Glory muffin.

"I know you drink tea, so that's what I got. And I looked at the size of these muffins and only got one. I can get a second if you don't want to share—or if we need to spend more time here."

"This is perfect," Rose said, and it was. She tore the muffin in half and bit into her piece. Still warm, it was chock full of fruit and nuts, and absolutely delicious. She could see why the Cakery was such a popular spot.

As they ate, they watched the crowd gradually dwindle until there was no one left to be served and only a few couples left at the tables. Rose and Murray left their crumbs and teacups and went up to the counter.

"Excuse me," Murray began. "We couldn't leave without telling you how marvelous that muffin was."

Samantha smiled, or rather, several planes in her face readjusted to form something resembling a smile. "I'm glad you enjoyed it. I hope you come back again."

She started to turn away but Rose stopped her. "We did have a question for you, if you don't mind."

Samantha stared at them blankly, but Eileen looked up from arranging a display of cupcakes. "Oh yes, they were in last week," she told Samantha. "They're Betsy's neighbors."

"I'm sure you've heard about Betsy by now," Rose said.

Samantha nodded once, brusquely. "The police were in earlier."

"Do you have any idea why she went to Newburgh?"

"I didn't know anything about her personal life. She was not a satisfactory employee from day one. I should have let her go the day I hired her."

"She was just so—weird," Eileen added. "She talked to herself and made up wild stories."

"What kind of stories?" Murray asked.

"Well, I told you about the serial killer," Eileen said. "And the cellist from the university that she believed was in love with her."

"Which he emphatically was not," Samantha cut in.

"Do you mean Greg?" Rose asked. "Did you know him personally?"

The two women looked at each other and burst out laughing, as if this were some sort of private joke.

"Well, I know he wanted nothing to do with Betsy," Eileen said when she could finally speak. "He has much better taste."

"And then there was that issue with the phone," Samantha went on. "She used to take pictures of the customers without their consent, which is obviously unacceptable. I told her to put it in the cloak room, but she wouldn't. Instead, she just carried it everywhere. All day long. As you can imagine, it's very difficult to box up a cake or carry platters of scones or even make change without setting your phone down."

"So what did she do?" Murray asked.

Eileen and Samantha exchanged glances again, this time accompanied by an eye roll.

"At first she tried putting it in her bra, but I nixed that," Samantha said. "Things were coming to a head, and if she hadn't—um, left—on her own, I'm sure I would have fired her quite soon."

Rose turned to Eileen. "You mentioned, I think, that she used to sit and stare at her phone during her lunch breaks. Was she texting?" She was quite proud of herself for even knowing what a text was.

"I can't imagine who would have texted her," Eileen said, looking at Samantha for confirmation.

"At least we know who wasn't," Samantha said, and Eileen smirked.

Justin suddenly appeared in their midst, wearing his Carhartt jacket again. "Excuse me, but it's ten," he said to Samantha. "I've got to go or I'll miss my bus."

"Are you going to the university?" Murray asked. "Let us drive you. We were going that way anyhow."

Justin's face flushed with relief. "Oh, sir, thank you so much. I'm always running late—it would be nice to get to class on time for once!"

And, thought Rose, it will be nice to talk to the only normal person in this shop!

Chapter Sixteen
Monday, February 9
10:00 a.m.

"Nice car," Justin said admiringly as he slipped into the back seat of Murray's Cadillac.

"Thanks," Murray said. "It's twelve years old but I keep it in tip-top shape. I do as much work on it myself as I can, and for the stuff I can't do, I have a mechanic who's worked on my cars for thirty years."

"Well, it shows," Justin said. "Someday I'd love to have a car like this."

"I hope you can," Murray said. "What's your major in school?"

"Business administration. I've already got a degree in culinary arts, but I want to open a bakery of my own, and I don't want to lose my shirt the first year like so many entrepreneurs do."

"Wise move," said Murray.

Rose had only the most skeletal idea about how Murray went from being a prosperous businessman to living entirely on Social Security. But she'd gotten the impression that his son David, Levi's father, had fallen victim to some risky investments and a sagging economy, taking Murray's fortunes down with him.

"Well, I have to think ahead," Justin said. "It isn't just about me. I've got a baby to support. Four months old. My wife works second-shift at the casino in Nichols, so she wakes me up when she comes home and I come down to the bakery to do the baking. I get to work about three a.m., leave work at ten and take two classes a day, five days a week. If we're lucky, Michelle and I might see each other for half a day on the weekend. And we won't even talk about how hard it is to keep up on my reading for class. But things will get better when I graduate."

"For sure," Rose said. "You're paying the price now but it will be worth it."

"What gets me," Justin went on, "is people who just seem to get everything handed to them. You know Eileen at the bakery? She majored in art in college—that and two bucks will buy you a cup of coffee. Samantha, who is like her best bud, enrolled her in some kind of cake-decorating course, so now Eileen considers herself a cake artist. She tells everyone she really doesn't need to work—her husband is a college professor—but my wife tells me that the famous Dr. Reeves blows his paycheck at the casino more nights than not. So Eileen might want to consider getting a real job—she just doesn't know it."

"Wait," Rose said. "She works at the Arts Council, doesn't she? Curating or something?"

"She only works two afternoons a week. Tuesdays and Thursdays. She's hardly in charge over there."

"So what's the deal with Samantha?" Rose asked. The university was only a few miles away, and Justin was proving to be such a storehouse of information, she wanted to get in every question she could. "The Cakery's been there forever, so she certainly isn't the first owner."

Justin shook his head. "She worked there for the Donaldsons in the nineties—when they retired, she and a woman named Vera took it over. This was when there was a real push to fund businesses owned by women. They had a hard time making a go of it at first, until the college started expanding downtown and the Cakery began selling lattes and bagels in addition to the more traditional stuff. Now it's a goldmine, and it's all due to Samantha." The admiration in his voice was plain.

"What happened to Vera?" asked Rose.

"Her husband wrote a best-selling book and left Vera for his publicist. So she moved west, closer to her children. Samantha and Eileen were already friends, so Samantha started grooming Eileen for Vera's spot. It's too bad Eileen doesn't give up this Arts Council fantasy and spend more time at the shop. Samantha's very active in the local business community—Rotary, Chamber of Commerce—and she needs somebody who can be at the shop all the time."

"And that wasn't Betsy," Murray observed.

"Betsy was an idiot. I'm sorry, I know she was your neighbor and you liked her and all, but as an employee she really wasn't worth the powder to blow her to Halifax, as my grandpa used to say. It took her forever to ring stuff up on the computer because she could barely remember how to use it from one day to the next."

"So she wasn't too good with technology," Rose said.

"That's putting it mildly," Justin said. "I'm not a computer geek by any means—that would have been Carl—but Betsy couldn't even find the app for Facebook after I downloaded it for her." He pointed out the window. "If you turn right and go around this big curve, you can let me out by the library."

"How did you know Carl?" Rose asked. This was just starting to get good; if she could have thought of a way to loop around the campus a few more times, she would have done it.

Justin slung his backpack over his shoulder, waiting for the right moment to exit. "When I first came to Binghamton, I roomed with Carl for a semester," he said. "We just weren't a good fit—he fit in better with Greg. But Carl sure did know his way around a computer, and he was always willing to help me out, so I can't fault the guy too much. This is my stop right here."

"Wait," Rose said. "What did you mean, he fit in better with Greg? Fit in how?"

Justin thought before he spoke. "With Carl, it was all about money, and he didn't have any scruples about how he got it. Greg is kind of the same way—I mean, we all know where his new cello came from, and what he did to get it."

"Where?" Rose asked, at the same time Murray asked "What?"

Justin opened the car door. "As to where, Samantha's purse. As to what—I'll let you figure that out. Anyway, thanks for the ride!"

With a friendly wave of his hand, Justin was gone.

Rose turned to Murray. "Samantha's purse?" she repeated in shock. "Greg and Samantha?"

"Curiouser and curiouser!" Murray said, veering into the visitor parking lot.

They retraced their steps to the music department office in the Fine Arts Building. This time a different student sat at the desk—a dark-haired girl with black lipstick and gauged ears.

"Can I help you?" she asked.

"Yes!" said Rose, a little too perkily, since she had absolutely no idea what she was going to say. She'd expected to rehearse with Murray on the way over to the university, but their conversation had gone in a different direction.

"We just stopped by to—that is, to—" Rose's gaze flitted frantically around the room, finally coming to rest on a poster advertising Saturday's concert. "We write for Senior Sunshine News—the senior citizens' paper—and we're

115

hoping to interview some of the students who will be performing in the concert this weekend. And we'd also like to find out if Greg Thomas is going to play a solo. So many of our readers are fans of his."

"Did you miss him in the fall concert?" the girl asked sympathetically. "A lot of people were really upset about that."

"We were in Florida then," Murray said smoothly. "I do seem to recall hearing that something happened, but I'm not sure what it was." He turned to Rose. "Do you remember, dear?"

She shook her head as if to dislodge the cobwebs from her brain. "No, I don't believe I do."

"It was catastrophic," the receptionist said, her black-rimmed eyes going wide. "Greg was scheduled to perform the cello solo in Bloch's *Schelomo*, and that afternoon, for some stupid reason, the police raided his apartment building and confiscated his computer and dragged him down to the police station for questioning."

"Why would they do that?" Murray asked. "Confiscate his computer? That seems really odd."

"I know, right? The police didn't find anything—I mean, he's not the type of guy to be into disseminating porn or building bombs for ISIS. He's terrifically talented and really only into music, which is all they found on his computer."

"Is that what they were looking for—porn or terrorism?" asked Rose.

"Well, no." The girl leaned forward. "Now, this is what I heard, but don't write it in the paper, and you didn't hear it from me." She swept her fingers across her mouth in a "zipped lip" motion. "There was a computer hacking case at Delaware Tech a few years ago—rumor is, the police were looking for evidence of something like that. But anybody who works here or goes to school with Greg could tell you that he couldn't hack up a hairball."

She giggled at her own joke, but since both Rose and Murray looked confused, she added, "He really doesn't know anything about computers, except for his music software and maybe Microsoft Word."

"Do you think it could have been his roommate's computer they were looking for?" Murray asked.

The girl looked surprised. "Greg had a roommate?"

"So what happened with the concert?" Murray asked. "Did he make it back in time to perform?"

"That was the catastrophe! By the time the police got done checking his hard drive and questioning him, it was past eight o'clock. The symphony couldn't perform the *Schelomo*, because they didn't have another cellist who could handle the part on such short notice, so the conductor had to substitute a different piece. The concert was okay, but people who were expecting to see Greg were really disappointed."

"Well, let's hope nothing like that happens next Saturday!" Rose said. "I would be devastated!"

Murray thanked the girl, grasped Rose's elbow firmly, and steered her into the hallway. "So much for asking his friends about Greg. 'Greg had a roommate?' she says. Feh!"

"So we bombed out with the Music Department," Rose said. "We hit pay dirt with Justin."

"True," Murray acknowledged. "Do you want to bum around the Computer Science building? We might run into some of Carl's friends there."

"Do you know where it is?"

"I think it's next to the library." Murray held the door so Rose could exit into the chilly February sunshine. "Every time you turn around, they've built a new building, but let's give it a shot."

Turning right outside the Fine Arts building, they walked along the western face of the Peace Quad and climbed a wide set of steps that took them to the library level. On the left-hand side of the enormous Library Tower, Murray paused in front of a small, relatively nondescript-looking brick building labeled "Technology Hub."

"I would have expected it to be bigger," he said doubtfully, but he held the door for Rose as they entered.

Just inside the door, a pleasant-looking young man was disemboweling a laptop. "Can I help you?" he asked.

"We're actually looking for the Computer Science department," Murray said. "Is this the right place?"

The young man chuckled. "No—this is just where you'd come for tech help. The big guns are in the Watson Engineering Building. You want to go right out there." He pointed his screwdriver toward a different set of glass doors that led outside again. "Head for the building that looks like a parking garage."

Following his directions, Murray and Rose were still surprised to see an enormous concrete structure that did look very much like a parking garage tucked alongside the library complex. They located the front door and found themselves stymied again.

Fortunately, a pretty young woman in an aqua hijab pointed them toward the elevator at the end of the hall. "You'll want to go to the second floor," she said.

"And then what?" Rose asked.

"And then you'll see a long hallway—oh, it's easier if I just show you."

The young woman got in the elevator with them and, once they'd reached their floor, escorted them to the

Computer Science office. It could not have been more different from the Music Department. No 1960s subway tile and oxidized aluminum windows here! The Wedgwood blue and brushed silver décor tastefully but unmistakably welcomed visitors to the twenty-first century. A chiseled young Asian man glanced up from one of the two reception desks, and Rose realized with a shock that he was the same young man she'd seen in the Music Department on their first visit there.

This time Murray had prepared an opening line. "Excuse me. Do you happen to know if there are any local services being planned for Carl Feinstein?"

The young man's eyes widened ever so slightly, and Rose noticed with surprise that today they were lime green. "Services?"

"Yes, I'm sorry," Murray persisted. "I couldn't reach his family and since he was a computer science major, I thought someone in the department might know. You did know Carl?"

"Everyone knew Carl." It wasn't an affirmation of sympathy, just a statement of fact.

"I thought that possibly if I could speak with one of his friends, someone might know whether there's a memorial service being planned, or a shiva house where we could mourn together."

The young man gave a peculiar shrug that seemed to shift a burden off his shoulder. "I'm not sure I know the answer to that question," he said at last. "Carl wasn't religious. He didn't hang out with people who were."

"Who did he hang out with?" Rose asked.

"Mostly the other GAs in the program. And Professor Reeves, obviously."

"Professor Reeves?" Rose gasped. "Brian Reeves?"

"Of course," the young man answered. "We're his graduate assistants, after all."

Chapter Seventeen
Monday, February 9
12:00 p.m.

Before leaving the university, Rose and Murray stopped at Brian Reeves' office in the Computer Science complex. The sign on his office door said the professor taught classes on Tuesday and Thursday mornings and held office hours on Mondays, Wednesdays and Fridays, but Murray's polite knock went unanswered. So he and Rose decided to head for Carl and Greg's apartment, since they really just wanted to talk to the neighbors.

Rose knew Carl's apartment building by reputation as well as by sight. Twin Georgian brick houses, mirror images of one another, had been converted to apartments some fifty years ago, and they had almost immediately attracted a succession of tenants of dubious repute. In the sixties, the rumors concerned pot parties and free love. In the seventies, it was cocaine; in the eighties, crack; in the nineties, heroin. Several years ago, a top-floor apartment was severely damaged by fire caused by a meth lab, and the city had threatened to lock the building down until a better class of tenants was obtained. The building was sold to a new management company, the damaged apartment was restored, and for a while it seemed that everything was under control—until the drug bust last year. Granted, the drug bust took place in the other building, not Carl's, but it had done nothing to improve the neighborhood's view of the twin Georgians.

Now the graceful architecture of the southernmost Georgian lady was marred by a boarded-up window facing Hesse Street—undoubtedly the window through which Carl had made his untimely exit. Rose clucked her tongue as she gazed at the buildings—not just for Carl, but for whoever had built those lovely structures back in the nineteenth century, full of optimism and hope, planning to house happy families.

"People have no respect," she said aloud.

"I know," Murray said. She looked across the front seat at him, surprised that he'd clearly been thinking the same thing.

They got out of the car and went up the front steps to the bank of mailboxes near the double glass doors. Feinstein/ Hopko lived in 3A; "Hopko" had been crossed out and "Thomas" written in small neat capitals above it. From the numbers on the mailboxes, there were three apartments on each of three floors. Murray tried the door to the foyer and found it unlocked, as Rose had expected it would be. This wasn't the type of building to have a security system.

On the third floor, they stopped outside apartment 3A and knocked loudly.

"Greg?" Murray shouted. "Greg, it's us! Get up, you lazy schlemiel!"

Rose giggled in spite of herself. Then she raised her own voice. "Maybe he's not there!"

"No, he's sleeping!" Murray banged on the door with his closed fist. "Greg, get up!"

Across the hall, the door to 3B opened, and a caramel-skinned man with enormous liquid brown eyes appeared.

"I don't think he's home," the man said, his accent Arabic and refined. "He studies at the university and often practices in the afternoons. He may not come back for hours."

Murray turned to Rose. "Maybe we could go to the college and find him there."

"Is there a problem?" asked the occupant of 3B.

Rose shook her head. "No, it's all right, Mr.—"

"Hussain. Asad Hussain."

"It's not all right," Murray said, shaking his head vigorously. "Carl was his roommate. Greg should have gone to the funeral. He's dishonored his friend."

"Perhaps there was a reason," Rose said. She turned to Asad. "Was there bad blood between Carl and Greg toward the end?"

Asad looked puzzled. "Bad blood?"

Murray banged his knuckles together, looking comically fierce. "Fighting."

Asad's eyes narrowed. "Why do you want to know?"

Murray shrugged. "It doesn't matter, I suppose. But Carl's parents said Greg didn't come to the funeral, and he didn't go to their home to pay his respects. I know he's practicing for his concert this weekend, but it is important to take time to honor the dead. I would just like to convince him to make peace with Carl's family."

Asad seemed to process this, and come to a decision. "Greg was not Carl's first roommate. When I moved here, Carl lived with Justin, nice man, who left to get married. Then Greg came and at first he and Carl got along well. But last fall the police came and arrested Greg when Carl was not home. They let Greg out later the same day, and he and Carl had a terrible row."

"Did you hear what they said?" Rose asked.

Asad held up his palm. "If I don't listen, I don't hear. If I don't hear, I can't testify. I told the police I was asleep with cold medicine."

"Who called the police?"

"Not me," said Asad. "To deal with the police is to ask for trouble."

"Did Carl and Greg fight often?"

"Greg is not a fighter," Asad said. "He is a musician, a lover. Except for that one time, he is not the one who fought with Carl."

"Who did?"

Asad shook his head. "If I do not open the door, I see nothing."

"If you don't tell us what you know," Murray said, "we see nothing."

Asad took a moment to process this as well. "The day Carl died, a man came to the house. I have heard him there before. It was not Greg, for sure—a different voice—an older man. Carl and the man began shouting, and I turned on the radio. They shout louder—I turn the radio up. Then the man left—I heard the door slam. Five minutes later, Carl shouted, 'Are you back again? I have nothing more to say to you!' and I decided it would be good for me to take a shower. When I came out of the bathroom, there were police everywhere. I made up my mind I would never, ever speak of it. I was in the shower, I said, and the radio was on. I heard nothing."

"But you did hear something," Rose pointed out. "Did you hear words? What did they say when they were shouting?"

Asad thought deeply. "A book," he said at last. "The man said, 'You have no right to the book.'"

"Thank you for telling us this," Murray said gently. "But why did you? You said you would never speak of it."

"You are not police. You remind me of my grandparents in Pakistan. And it was so terrible. I had to tell someone."

They left Asad and made their way back to the car. Rose took a long look at the building as they drove away; it was too sad, that beautiful Georgian lady with her eye patched shut, and all the terrible history contained within her walls.

"Who do you think was the man who argued with Carl?" Rose asked Murray. "And they argued about a book? Who does that?"

"I can't imagine," Murray said. "But I'm exhausted, and I need to go to sleep. Ask me in about three hours."

"Come for ziti at five," Rose suggested. "You can have ziti, right, if I don't put cheese and meat in the same dish?" The corners of Murray's mouth turned up just the tiniest bit. "Remember, I said we wouldn't worry about it," he told her. Rose had the feeling there was more that he'd elected not to say.

*   *   *

At five o'clock sharp, Murray was back at the door of Rose's apartment, rapping out his familiar "shave and a haircut—two bits" knock. She'd made a salad, of course, and toasted her own croutons under the broiler after taking out her delicious vegetarian ziti. She'd forgotten to buy garlic bread, so she baked refrigerator crescent rolls and coated them in a mixture of olive oil and garlic. Her Italian mother, who had made everything from scratch, would have been scandalized, but even in retirement Rose had better things to do than knead bread when such nice alternatives were available.

Rose poured each of them a goblet of grape juice. Then she scooped out a huge portion of steaming ziti for Murray and one almost as big for herself, tucking a roll beside each.

"May I say grace?" Murray asked, a twinkle in his eye.

"Go ahead," Rose said, surprised.

Murray extracted a yarmulke from his pocket, put it on his head, and picked up his dinner roll. "Blessed are you,

125

Lord our God, King of the universe, who brings forth bread from the earth. Amen."

Rose noticed that he pronounced "Amen" as if it were spelled "Ah-main." She decided there was nothing in that grace that she could object to in the least and made the sign of the cross to seal her conviction.

Murray picked up his wine glass and clinked it against hers. "L'chaim!"

"Salute!" Rose responded.

Rose laid her steno pad on the table before digging eagerly into her supper; she was happy to see that Murray dug in just as enthusiastically. The ziti really was delicious—hollow ribbed pasta in chunky tomato sauce with mushrooms, green peppers and onions, striated throughout with a mixture of mozzarella and ricotta cheeses. Her quick-fix garlic bread was also a hit. It took at least five minutes of serious eating before they could slow down sufficiently to talk about the case.

"So who was the man who fought with Carl the day he died?" Rose asked.

"I think right now, the best we can do is say who it wasn't," Murray answered, dabbing his mouth with his napkin. "It wasn't Justin, because Asad would have recognized his voice. Ditto Greg. So for now that's a dead end. I think we should focus on what we do know."

"Okay," Rose said. "Last fall, on the night of the symphony concert, there was some kind of police investigation that resulted in Greg being brought in for questioning. They confiscated his computer. No charges were brought against him and they let him go, but he fought with Carl later that night. What's going on there?"

Murray added this to Rose's steno pad. "Carl helped Justin with his computer. So Carl was the one who was good with computers, not Greg. But the police took Greg's computer, not Carl's, which makes me suspect that Carl knew they were coming and kept his computer off-site. Now, what else do we know about Greg? Betsy was in love with him, but he pretty much saw her as a stalker. He had dated Betsy's sister Sara in high school."

"Is Sara in love with him too? I mean still?"

"I don't know," Murray said. "You talked to her—I didn't."

"We'll write that down as a question that still needs to be answered," Rose said. "And here's another thing we know about Greg—Samantha bought him a new cello."

"I got that from Justin's remark. But why would she do that?" Murray asked.

Rose gave him a look. "Why do you think? I know he's twenty-three and she's got to be forty, but it happens in the tabloids all the time."

"But the only person who even hinted at this was Justin, unless you want to include those weird undercurrents between Samantha and Eileen," Murray said reasonably. "We've got to be able to confirm it through some other source before we start accusing Samantha of being a cheetah."

"Cougar," Rose corrected. "And I've got another question. Betsy apparently had no idea how to use her Smartphone—but nevertheless, she spent all her lunch hours and breaks playing with it, and was terrified someone would steal it. What's up with that?"

"That I really don't understand," Murray said. "But then I don't know much about Smartphones. My son and grandson have them, and you can do anything with them—go on the internet and watch movies, you name it. The younger people would be the ones to ask."

"We need to talk to a lot of people," Rose observed. "And not just about phones! We need to talk to the Feinsteins about their relationship with their son. I need to talk to Eileen about her husband's relationship with Carl, and you need to talk to Samantha about Greg—trust me, Samantha would talk to you better than she would me. Could you talk her up at a Rotary meeting?"

"Rotary's on Tuesday morning, and I have a doctor's appointment at eleven and lunch with David afterward. Besides, I haven't belonged to Rotary for years."

Rose bustled across the room toward the phone. "The meetings aren't on Tuesday, they're on Wednesday now, and my friend Cookie's husband can get you in as a guest. Just tell them you're opening a bookstore."

"Why a bookstore?" Murray asked.

"Because that's what a nice Jewish man with a bow tie would open," Rose said, half a second before Cookie came on the line. "Cookie? I've got a favor to ask—"

Chapter Eighteen
Tuesday, February 10
12:00 p.m.

Rose knew that Eileen didn't start her job at the Broome County Arts Council until afternoon, so she killed time in the morning by setting up the sewing machine on the desk in her bedroom and working on a new dress. She'd fallen in love with the fabric over a year ago at a shop in Syracuse, but at the time she bought it, she had no idea where she'd ever wear anything so elegant. Now, with the symphony concert coming up in only five days, she hoped she'd have time to finish it.

At noon, she folded up her sewing, put on her coat and hat, and went downstairs to wait for the bus. She had never learned to drive and normally didn't miss it, but having Murray as a chauffeur for the last week had spoiled her. There was no way she'd be able to go as many places in a single day as she'd been able to do in a car—but on the other hand, there was no way she'd have been able to figure out so much of this case without Murray. Staring out the grimy window of the bus, she knew that as much as she missed driving around in Murray's Cadillac, she missed Murray more.

At last the bus came to a stop on the corner of Court and Washington, Rose alighted and squared her shoulders. She didn't need to tote Murray along just to question Eileen. She had this. She walked east on Court Street until she reached State and turned right towards the Stephens Square building which housed the Arts Council.

On the fifth floor, she entered a small, charming office with wood floors, chestnut woodwork, and oriental rugs.

Eileen sat in front of a computer, swathed in an enormous pashmina, her long earrings swinging as she typed; she looked up pleasantly to greet the newcomer and her expression abruptly darkened.

"Why, Mrs. Bevelacqua," she said stiffly. "I didn't know you supported the arts."

"I don't, really," Rose said. "Although I do quilt. And I make clothes. But you know that's not why I'm here. I have a few questions."

Eileen sighed. "Well, let's make it snappy. I'm working on a mailing list that has to be done by the end of the week. And Thursday I have to work all day at the bakery, training a temp girl Samantha's bringing in from an agency to fill Betsy's spot, so I'm not going to have a chance to work on the mailing list after today."

"I won't keep you long," Rose said. "It's just that you know so many things that I couldn't get from anyone else, and I really want to find out what happened to Betsy. I told her sister I'd try and find some explanation, and I owe her that."

"If her sister is as dumb as Betsy was, I wish you luck explaining anything to her."

Rose swallowed a thousand possible replies. "I realized when I talked to you before, I never asked anything about you. For example, I think you mentioned that you're married—."

Eileen extended her left hand, nearly bowing under the weight of a showy diamond ring. "My husband Brian is a professor at Binghamton University. I met him when he was in grad school at Columbia and I was an undergraduate there. He's got a brilliant future—his book on statistical systems analysis won the Schermerhorn Prize last year, and he's only thirty-eight."

"Mmm," said Rose appreciatively. She had no idea what statistical systems analysis was.

"When I married Brian, I was working in New York as a sculptor," Eileen went on. "That's my real passion—sculpture. Would you like to see the piece I've completed for the First Friday exhibit?"

"I'd love to," Rose said insincerely.

Rose followed her into a small workroom off the front office. There, Eileen proudly showed off a terra cotta sculpture that looked like a swirly pile of reddish-brown custard, or somewhat off-color poop.

"It's—astonishing," Rose said, which fortunately Eileen seemed to take as a compliment. "I can see why you like decorating cakes."

"I work at the Cakery because there I can create edible art," Eileen went on, returning to the reception desk. "At the shop I get the chance to practice my technique every day. I don't need the paycheck, of course—Brian obviously makes more than enough money to support us both—but it's important to keep my sculpting muscles toned. Brian won't be in Binghamton forever, and I want to return to my career someday."

"I'd heard that Samantha wanted you to be a full partner in the shop."

Eileen's chin hiked a little higher, if possible. "Of course I respect Samantha tremendously, and I'm pleased that she appreciates my contribution to her little shop. But I would never do that. I have an obligation to my muse, and of course, to the Binghamton arts community."

"So where were you when Betsy was killed?"

"That was when—Saturday?" Eileen asked.

"Thursday morning, they think."

"Thursday morning I was at the shop, obviously, because Betsy wasn't." Suddenly she looked mischievous. "But I'll bet you don't know who wasn't where he said he was going to be."

"Who?"

"Justin," said Eileen triumphantly.

Rose tilted her head, puzzled. "Justin said he goes to school every weekday at ten."

"And most days he probably does. But I happen to know that on Thursday, he didn't. At eleven-thirty, he was downtown getting takeout at China Star."

"That actually proves he wasn't in Newburgh, you know. It proves he was in Binghamton."

Eileen sighed. "Look. You may think I'm prejudiced, but as much as I admire Justin for working to rise out of the hood, there's no point. It's nice that Carl made time to help Justin with his schoolwork, but Justin's just a Polish kid from Johnson City. He doesn't have the background to make something of himself. I'm surprised, actually, that he does so well at a challenging school like BU; maybe he has other helpers besides just Carl. Some people just aren't meant to be one of us, and Justin isn't. On the other hand, take Carl, who was a brilliant mathematician, and Greg, who is a brilliant musician. Those are the people you'd want to help because they deserve it, and they're going to use their talents to achieve greatness rather than just manage a shop. Helping them isn't charity—it's an investment in the future."

Rose, who had grown up in the Little Italy section of Endicott, felt her blood throbbing in her veins. But this was not the time to get into an argument with a bigot. "Did someone support Carl and Greg?" she asked.

Eileen twisted the corner of her lips, clearly trying to decide the possible ramifications of saying something she very much wanted to say. Finally she caved. "Samantha has sort of taken Greg under her wing. Now you didn't hear that from me. He is so talented, and she has very highly-placed contacts in New York City because she used to live and work there. She got him some wonderful gigs—he played Carnegie Hall at Christmastime—and then of course, in order to be competitive with professional musicians, he needed a very expensive cello and Samantha fronted the money for that. As well as securing some additional training that wouldn't have been available in Binghamton."

"And what does Samantha get in return for her—generosity?"

"Why, nothing!" Eileen seemed sincerely surprised by the question. "She's very fond of him, of course, and he of her. They spend a lot of time together. But there's no contract between them. He doesn't have to pay her back—her reward is in knowing the part she played in his success."

Rose remembered the looks Eileen and Samantha had exchanged at the Cakery, and she knew better. "And who was supporting Carl?"

Eileen readjusted her pashmina. "Did I say someone was supporting Carl? I believe I said they should have, not that they did. He came from a poor family—his father was a public school teacher—so he didn't have much, but his parents are obviously cultured people and he'd obtained a research fellowship here, and my husband believed that eventually Carl's brilliance would have taken him far in academia. His death was a tragedy."

"And Betsy's wasn't?"

"Betsy was a sad case. You were her neighbor, weren't you? So you know. I don't think she'd ever had a proper haircut. I don't think she'd ever been to the dentist. I can't imagine how she graduated from high school. I'm not even

133

sure how she got out of sixth grade. A ten-year-old knows when her clothes don't match. A ten-year-old knows how to use a cell phone. A ten-year-old can tell stories with some basis in reality."

Something fluttered in Rose's memory, but it flashed out again so quickly she couldn't attach words to it. "We keep coming back to Betsy's phone," she said. "Betsy didn't use it the way other people do. She didn't text, she didn't go online, she didn't use Facebook. But both you and Justin said that she played with it for her entire lunch hour, she wouldn't let it out of her hands, and she was terrified it would get stolen. Do you have any idea why she would have this obsession with her phone?"

"Of course," Eileen said. "It was that pathetic crush she had on Greg Thomas! She'd turn handsprings to get a selfie with him, and then she'd spend her whole lunch hour mooning over the photos on her phone. I'm sorry the poor girl got murdered and I can't imagine why anyone would kill her. But she was an idiot. She really wasn't worth all the effort you're putting into finding out what happened to her."

"That's not true," Rose said. "She was a child of God. Everybody is worth the effort of finding out the truth."

Eileen shot her nose into the air. "You're entitled to your own opinion, I'm sure. Now I really have to get back to work."

Rose was more than ready to let her.

Back on Court Street Rose waited for the bus, and it seemed much colder now than it had an hour ago when she'd made the trip downtown. Rose now knew Betsy wasn't lying about her phone—she really didn't do Facebook or Instagram or Twitter—she only made calls and took pictures, and the pictures were mainly of Greg. Sara had said that Betsy had come to Binghamton because Greg was in grad school here. Betsy must have thought that if she had him all to herself, without Sara, he would eventually reciprocate her love. But that implied that he was still in love with Sara —or that Betsy thought he was, and it might have gone both ways. Sara might be more involved in this than Rose had thought.

She could hardly wait to tell Murray, but that could wait for the following morning; she had a couple of questions to ask Diane and Parker first, and she'd always found it most effective to bribe her girls with food.

She'd just have to make a quick stop at Price Chopper on the way back to her apartment.

Chapter Nineteen
Tuesday, February 10
5:30 p.m.

Diane and Parker rented a 1980s duplex in Endwell, about ten miles west from Rose's apartment building. Their house had that clean, well-kept, but ultimately antiseptic feel of people who don't have enough time to make their house a home. More distressingly for Rose, it was nearly a mile off the bus line, which made it extremely difficult to just drop in on her family unannounced. But Rose didn't like calling ahead; it felt too much like she was making an appointment to see her own child. So on Tuesday at about five-thirty, she toted an enormous soft-sided cooler onto the bus, through Diane's neighborhood, and up her front steps, setting it down momentarily to knock politely before walking in.

The door was locked.

Diane often only locked her front door when she went out or retired for the night, although Parker generally locked it when she was home alone. Leaving her cooler on the porch, Rose checked the garage window, and her worst fears were confirmed: the car was gone. She knew that if she went next door, Sophie Stacconi would drive her home. But it was such an inconvenience to ask someone who wasn't even family. She wavered in front of the garage, as if by force of sheer will she could summon Diane's car back home.

"Nonni? What are you doing out there in the driveway?"

She followed the sound of the familiar voice and saw Parker's face in the kitchen window.

"Where's your mother?" Rose responded, using her hand to shield her eyes from the setting sun.

"Oh, thank you for being so happy to see me!" Parker teased. "It's great to see you too, Nonni, especially when it looks like you've brought dinner."

"Beans and greens with sausage," Rose said.

"Mmm, I love beans and greens and sausage!" The curtains dropped over the windowpane, and in ten seconds Parker appeared on the front stoop. She scurried down the front steps to help her grandmother with the insulated tote. "Did you bring garlic bread?"

"There's a baguette in there, sliced in two crosswise," Rose answered, passing Parker on the stoop and heading for a kitchen chair. "Man alive! Couldn't your mother have found a house a little closer to a bus stop?"

"She's trying, but she just hasn't found anything she likes," Parker said. "How come no garlic bread?"

"The garlic bread comes frozen and it would have made the casserole cold. Where *is* your mother?"

Parker carefully lifted the casserole from the tote. "Wow, it's still screaming hot—I almost couldn't pick it up. I'll cut the bread and pour us some juice. Mom's at her book club. First Tuesday of the month."

"Oh, phooey." Rose knew the library's book club meetings were notorious for spilling over into the nearest pub and running close to midnight.

"It's great you brought beans and greens," Parker said, setting out two wide bowls and framing them with silverware and napkins. "That means we won't need a salad. Are we saying grace?"

"You and your grace," Rose said, filling her bowl with steaming goodness. "I'm an old woman. I need to be fed."

They were both silent for a while, except for an occasional "mmm" or "ahhh" of satisfaction. When Parker finished her first bowl, Rose pushed the casserole dish closer to her granddaughter and Parker didn't need to be asked twice. She reciprocated when her grandmother got down to the last bean or two at the bottom of her own bowl.

Just as they were finishing dinner, Parker's cell phone buzzed, and she glanced at the screen.

"Nonni, do you mind if I take this? It's about homework, it really is."

"Go ahead," Rose said.

Parker swiped her finger across the screen, said hello, and began listening. After a moment, she said, "I think it's a great idea, but I don't think you can access that site without a password. Do you know anyone who is already a subscriber?"

The chatter continued on the other end of the phone as Rose took the dishes to the sink.

Parker interrupted. "Do you have a library card? Great. Go to the library website and click on research center—sometimes it's called databases. You might be able to access that site through them."

She took the phone away from her ear and began tapping and scrolling, continuing to talk at the same time. "It looks like there are two levels of access—if you want the most detailed information, you'd have to be in the library to get that, but there's still a lighter version of the program you can use at home."

Parker put the phone back up to her ear, listening to her caller. Finally she said, "I think you're on the right track. My grandmother's visiting, so I don't want to stay on the phone too long, but if you have any other questions, call me back."

She tapped the phone and put it in her back pocket.

Rose stared at her in astonishment. "Did you just look something up—like information—on your phone?" she asked.

Parker nodded. "My study partner is trying to figure out whether two signers of the Declaration of Independence were related, and she thought maybe a genealogy site would help. I just showed her where to find one."

"On your phone."

"Well, she's going to use *her* phone to look something up in the library research center."

"Could you use your phone to find me something that may have been in the news a couple of years ago?"

"It depends on what it is," Parker said. "A classified ad, no. A building catching on fire or a major flood, probably."

"What about this? At a college called Delaware Tech, someone was arrested for breaking into professor's computers and stealing exam answers."

"Hacking," Parker said. She brought up Google and typed "Delaware Tech hacking exam" into the search box. Immediately a string of results filled the page, and Rose moved in closer so she could see the tiny screen. "There's a lot on it. Even made the *New York Times*."

"Impressive," Rose said.

Parker suddenly looked puzzled. "Wait. The Delaware hacking happened almost three years ago. The *New York Times* article was written two years later. Let's look at that." More tapping and sweeping brought up the *New York Times* article. "Aha. In the original hacking case at Delaware Tech, a guy hacked into a professor's computer to get the answers to an exam, and then two other guys sold them to students enrolled in the course. But in that instance, it was just one exam, one professor, and a couple of guys who weren't smart enough to avoid getting caught."

"Don't let Uncle Vincent hear you say that," Rose said.

Parker ignored her. "But two years later, the *New York Times* reported that a plot had been uncovered to do something similar, but on a much bigger scale, involving not just one professor and one exam but the whole state university system. And it would have required not just one hacker but whole teams of them on each campus, with a secret campus coordinator. The guy at the top was a computer science professor named Simon McKendrick, from a college on Long Island."

"Long Island," Rose said. "Interesting."

"Yup. Anyway, McKendrick was caught this past December before he had the chance to do much damage, and now the authorities are trying to track down all his accomplices before they try it again."

"This past December?"

"Yes. Christmas break. Why? What does this have to do with your case?"

"I'm not sure," Rose said. "But I have a couple of other things I want you to do for me. First, you remember you said you couldn't see much of Greg's Facebook page because it was private?"

Parker nodded. "Most people's are."

"But if you were a friend of his, you could see it, right?"

"Well, it depends on what you mean by being his friend. If you know him personally but you're not on Facebook, you can't see his page just by clicking on it. You have to ask Greg if he wants you to be his Facebook friend—he has to accept you."

"Hmm," Rose said. "What about that thing the President uses—Tweeter? Is that the one where you exchange pictures?"

"The pictures are Instagram," Parker corrected. "And tweets come from Twitter. Again, it depends on whether Greg's account is public or private. But on Twitter most people's accounts are public, and anyone can follow them."

"So I can sign up to follow Greg?"

"You don't have a Smartphone."

"Do I need one?" Rose asked.

"If you're going to use Twitter or Instagram, yes, it helps," Parker explained. "I've heard of people who tweet from their computer, but it's really a Smartphone thing. And really, Greg *is* hot, but you're a little old for him." At Rose's incredulous look, Parker played innocent. "What? I've seen his picture on Instagram. He's hot."

"Then could *you* get on his Twitter list?" Rose suggested. "And his Instagram list, or whatever. And then you can tell me what he says, and where he goes, and who he's with—"

"Wait, wait, noooo. That's creepy."

"Look," Rose said. "I just want to find out who killed Betsy, and if Carl really was murdered and by whom. Carl had a crush on Betsy. Betsy had a crush on Greg. Only one of those three people is still alive. If you can keep Greg alive, wouldn't you want to?"

"I hadn't thought about it like that," Parker said. She pondered a minute, then gave a single decisive nod. "I'll do it. Only I'm not going to, like, follow him to the bathroom."

"Well, I would hope he wouldn't be taking pictures in the bathroom!"

"You'd be surprised." Parker clicked and tapped and swiped and then nodded her head again. "Twitter and Instagram--done. Now, do you want to watch *Downton Abbey*? I'll make popcorn. And when Mom gets back, she can drive you home."

"Sounds great," Rose said, suspecting she'd be curled up on the couch for a good long time.

Chapter Twenty
Wednesday, February 11
9:00 a.m.

On Wednesday morning, Rose woke up especially early, excited to learn whether Murray was able to talk to Samantha at the Rotary breakfast, and eager to share what she'd learned from her visit with Parker. She jumped into the shower, vigorously scrubbing shampoo into and out of her short grey hair, and even adding a touch of makeup to her usual facial routine. She augmented her body lotion with the tiniest spritz of cologne, and put on the pretty pink top Murray had admired with the black pressed slacks she usually wore to funerals. As a final touch, she took out her standard gold stud earrings and substituted little pearls. She checked herself in the mirror—not bad, she decided, for seventy-four.

She hurried out to the kitchen, put on the teakettle, and chose a box of especially fragrant tea Diane had given her for Christmas. Murray would already have had breakfast when he arrived, but he might like a little something to go along with his tea, so she broke into a new box of chocolate-dipped biscotti, fanning them out on the plate just the way they did on the cooking shows. Then she transferred her teabags into a delicate china tea pot and covered them with boiling water, delighting in the amazing spicy scent. When she heard someone in the hallway, she checked herself in the living room mirror one more time before opening the door.

"Oh," she said. "It's you."

Vincent tossed his coat onto the living room sofa and sniffed the air. "What's that smell?"

"I made a different kind of tea," she said. "I was running low on the usual kind."

Her son followed his nose into the kitchen. His eyes traveled from the beautifully-presented biscotti to Rose's pink top and pearl earrings. "You're definitely expecting someone, and I don't think it's me."

"None of your business," she told him.

"Well, here's something that's none of *your* business," he responded, his dark eyes flashing. "Didn't I tell you not to get involved in a police investigation?"

"What makes you think I have?"

"Why else would my niece suddenly follow Greg Thomas on Instagram and Twitter? I have a hard time believing she's suddenly switched from hip hop to classical music."

"Maybe she has," Rose said airily. "You know teenagers—one minute it's crash-boom-bah, and the next it's Pavarotti."

"And is Murray Zimmerman planning to take Parker to the university symphony on Saturday? If so, maybe I'd better start looking at *him*."

"How did you know—" Rose began, and then realized he'd caught her. "One of those tickets, I'll have you know, is for me."

"You have a date with Murray Zimmerman?"

"We're friends, yes."

"Seriously? You got hysterical when I took Rama Patel to dinner because she wasn't Catholic."

"Well, I've changed," Rose said flatly. "Does your visit have a point, other than to harass me about my choice of companion?"

"Yes," Vincent answered. "I don't give a flying fig who you date—well, I do, but Murray seems like a nice guy. But

I care very much when you plunge into the middle of a double homicide investigation, and get my niece involved as well. Did it ever occur to you that you might be putting your granddaughter in danger?"

"I would never do that!"

"Ma, you don't get it. You *have* done it, and you are continuing to do it. Just stop. Please. Make a quilt. Hook a rug. Take up yoga. For everyone's sake."

"Should I tell Parker to defriend Greg?"

"Unfriend, and that only applies to Facebook. I think that would attract more attention than just leaving things as they are. Just tell Parker that you're sorry you put her in this position and to ignore any tweets she receives from Greg— unless they're disturbing, in which case she should report them to me. Not you."

At that moment the front door opened, and Murray walked through the living room into the kitchen. He wore a beautiful grey pinstripe suit with a light blue shirt and a silk bow-tie of a slightly deeper hue, and he was carrying a plastic sack of bagels. Vincent looked him up and down and up again.

"Going somewhere?" he asked.

Murray smiled pleasantly. "I thought I might take your mother to breakfast."

"Then what's with the bagels?" Vincent began, then cut himself off. "Never mind. Not my business. Have a nice— whatever."

From the living room, he called back, "But Ma—you remember what I told you."

After the door slammed, Murray said, "Did I come at a bad time?"

Rose shook her head. "Vincent thinks we should stop sleuthing. I accidentally involved Parker last night, Vincent

144

got wind of it, and he came to make sure I didn't do it again."

"Then maybe you don't want to hear about my conversation with Samantha."

"Like heck I don't," Rose said. "Sit down, let me pour you some tea, and would you like a biscotti?"

"Try and stop me," Murray said.

They settled down at the breakfast table. Rose put both elbows on the table and leaned forward, which made Murray chuckle.

"Your friend Lou met me at the door—turns out I knew him from years back, when I owned the furniture store and he worked for the paper. I gave him the line you suggested— I'm considering opening a bookstore, which the more I think about it seems like a really intriguing idea."

"Aren't you a little old to be starting a business?" Rose asked. "You were just supposed to be chatting up Samantha."

"I'm eighty-four, thank you very much, and Samantha and I did have a nice little chat. In fact, it worked out really well—Lou actually introduced me to her, I reminded her we'd already met, and when she chose a seat, I just followed and sat down beside her. She mentioned needing to get back to the shop because they're shorthanded. She didn't even pretend to feel bad about poor Betsy. Mostly she seemed annoyed because until they hire someone else, staffing will be a nightmare. Not, she said, that Betsy had been a terrific employee—in fact she was practically useless. So I asked her why she'd kept her on so long."

"That's been bothering me, too," Rose said.

Murray reached for a second biscotti. "Apparently Betsy was hired as part of a training program for people with mild disabilities, and Samantha got reimbursed for keeping her on for six months. When the reimbursement money stopped, Samantha would have had to pay her minimum wage out of her own pocket, which she had no intention of doing. She'd planned to tell the agency that Betsy hadn't been a very satisfactory employee, the agency would have sent somebody else, and Betsy would have been out on the street."

"That's the first explanation that makes sense."

"Samantha said that when she agreed to hire Betsy, she assumed that any warm body could run a cash register. She quickly discovered that wasn't true. Before long, Samantha felt Betsy was beginning to annoy the customers—striking up inappropriate conversations, taking pictures of them when they were reading or chatting with friends or sharing a personal moment. She says she tried to speak to Betsy about it, but Betsy didn't seem to understand how her behavior impacted the regulars."

"And speaking of Greg," Rose said dryly, "did Samantha mention him? Anything that might support Justin's theory that he and Samantha were having an affair?"

"Not a word—and I tried, believe me. As a segue into discussing Greg and Carl, I did ask her if she knew any of Betsy's friends, but Samantha claimed she didn't fraternize with the help *or* the customers, so that was a dead end. What she really wanted to discuss were the expenses Betsy's death have caused her. The agency that placed Betsy at the Cakery takes several weeks to select and prepare a new candidate, which doesn't help Samantha right now. She's bringing someone in from a temp agency today, at almost twice what she'd paid Betsy. She has to take time out of her busy schedule to train the temp. And someone came in yesterday to buy a pre-decorated birthday cake and wanted Eileen to add an inscription on top, but Eileen was taking a phone order and the birthday boy got exasperated and left. None of which, apparently, would have happened if they'd had a designated counter girl."

"Her compassion is touching," Rose said.

"Isn't it though?" Murray agreed. "It took me a good ten minutes to turn her around to discussing the other staff members. Samantha knows Eileen sucks up to her and she uses it to her full advantage. Justin—well, he's a great baker, the best she's ever had, but the fact that he can only work that narrow schedule limits his usefulness. She puts up with it because she's hoping to hire him full time when he graduates from college. And then she told me, in excruciating detail, about her essential roles in the Chamber, and Rotary, and the Junior League, and every other organization you could throw a stick at. But that did net one helpful bit of information."

"What?"

"On the day Carl died, Samantha claims she never left the bakery until late afternoon, when she set up for a Chamber mixer at the Doubletree. Given that she claims to be essential to every function of the Chamber of Commerce, that should be easy to check. And on Thursday around noon—when Betsy was killed—Samantha was in full view of the lunchtime crowd at the bakery. She wasn't in Newburgh, and she's got lots of witnesses to attest to that."

"Bummer," Rose said, inadvertently using an expression she'd picked up from Parker. "She was such an agreeable murderer."

"Absolutely," Murray agreed. "I wish she could have done it too."

The phone rang, and they both jumped. Rose pushed herself to her feet and grabbed the cordless handset.

"Mrs. Bevelacqua?" A young voice, familiar somehow. "This is Sara Mangero."

"Oh, yes, Sara," Rose said, hiking her eyebrows at Murray. "I haven't made any progress. At least, I've learned a lot but I haven't put the pieces together."

"That's okay," Sara said. "I know you're trying. I really just wanted to tell you that I'm having Betsy's body cremated, and I'm coming out to Binghamton to pick up the ashes on Friday. I wondered if you could let me into Betsy's apartment when I come out. Most of the stuff can probably go to Goodwill, but there are a half-dozen things I know I'd like to keep."

Rose started to tell Sara that she didn't have a key, but she stopped herself. "Sure," she said. "There's no caution tape across the door, so I don't see a problem with that. Just call me as soon as you get into town."

She said good-bye and hung up, turning to find Murray staring at her in frank admiration.

"Breaking and entering, not once but twice," he said. "Contaminating a crime scene. Lying to the police. Interfering with a police investigation. Definitely my kind of gal."

Chapter Twenty-One
Thursday, February 12
7:00 a.m.

In Rose's dream, she was sitting in the old blue Chrysler outside the Pig Stand with Dom, eating pork sandwiches wrapped in greasy paper. Dom had just reached toward her to get a French fry when suddenly a fire engine rushed by, and then another, and then another. It was only on the fourth ring that Rose realized it was the telephone, opened her eyes, and grabbed the receiver.

"Rose?"

"Murray Zimmerman," she croaked. "It is much too early to call people. "

"I know, but this is important. I asked Sol to call me when the Feinsteins left their house, and they just did."

"What are you talking about?"

"The Feinsteins. Carl's parents. They live in Sol's neighborhood, remember? He saw them pull out of their driveway, which means they're not sitting shiva any more. He figures they're on their way to Binghamton."

Rose took a sip of water to clear her throat. "How far away is Tarrytown?"

"About three hours."

"So they could be here at—" she looked her hand-wound Big Ben "—ten o'clock?"

"Theoretically. They might stop to stretch their legs, but if they don't, they could be here as early as ten."

"So pick me up at nine-thirty. We'll head them off at the pass. And if we play our cards right, we'll get a chance to see the inside of Carl's apartment."

149

After hanging up, Rose threw off the covers and tottered into the bathroom, cursing her morning arthritis. She slapped some deodorant under her arms, brushed her teeth and hair, and dressed quickly in somber colors. Rose didn't know what sort of clothing would be appropriate for a Jewish sympathy call, but she couldn't imagine it would be much different from a Catholic one.

Then she toasted a leftover bagel, applied a "schmear" of cream cheese, poured a strong cup of tea, and waited.

Two and a half hours had never passed so slowly. After finishing her breakfast, reading the paper, hemming her new jacket, and struggling to get interested in a library book, Rose gave up and turned on a morning talk show. After a very handsome man explained how to organize a closet and a perky little thing made lamb ratatouille, Murray finally knocked on the front door.

"Hope I'm not too early," he said. "You sounded a little sleepy on the phone."

"That was a lifetime ago," Rose said, grabbing her coat and purse and pulling the door shut behind her.

It only took a few minutes to get to Carl's apartment building. And then outside Carl's building, they waited again. Except this time, Rose felt like a cat waiting to pounce.

"There are too many parts to this mystery," she said, nervously tapping her nails on the door handle.

"You know, I really don't think there are," Murray said. "There are Moby Dick questions, and little red herrings. We just don't know one from the other yet. We don't know who the silver-eyed man is—"

"I do," Rose said. "It's the Asian student in the Computer Science department. The first time we saw him, his eyes were brown—their normal color. The second time we saw him, they were bright lime green. Nobody has lime eyes. So he knows where to buy novelty contacts and he's comfortable wearing them."

"But why?" Murray asked. "Okay, he's a graduate student who knows Carl, and it doesn't sound like they were best buddies. But why would he dress up in costume and buy a cake?"

"I think they actually might have been a lot closer than our Asian friend was willing to let on. When we asked him about Carl, he shut down. That's not really the sign of a person who doesn't care at all—it's the sign of a person who doesn't want to talk about it." Rose sighed. "But I don't see the point of pretending to be a serial killer in the first place. And we don't know why he would put a dead cat behind the bakery."

"Or even if he was the one who did it," Murray reminded her. "All of those things were intended to scare Betsy. But why?"

"Would you stop saying that?" Rose scolded. "Why. Why. We don't know why."

"True," Murray said. "We don't. And we don't know why Carl was so desperate to get Betsy out of Binghamton. We don't know who was fighting with Carl when he went out the window. Or whether the relationship between Greg and Samantha is significant. Or how the hacking scheme fits in. And we don't know why Betsy was so paranoid about her phone—"

"There they are!" Rose cried abruptly.

A black Honda Accord parallel-parked in front of them. The frame around the license plate read "Tarrytown Honda." Two people alighted, a dark-haired woman in jeans and a leather jacket, and a man in a short wool coat. At first glance the woman appeared too young to be the mother of a college student, but on second glance, her age appeared in the way she carried herself. Rose's mother had a replica of Michaelangelo's *Pieta* sitting on the mantel, and this woman, this Jewish mother of a dead son, had the same look of grief that knew no bounds.

Murray swung the car door open, "Mr. Feinstein!"

The woman's husband turned around—a small, trim man with wire-rimmed glasses. "I am Ira Feinstein," he said. "Do I know you?"

Murray moved forward much more rapidly than Rose would have thought possible. "Murray Zimmerman," he said. "Sol Cohen is a dear friend of mine. And I—we—wanted to extend our deepest sympathies on the loss of your son."

"Thank you," Ira said. He moved around the car, closer to the tragic woman. "This is my wife Esther. Carl's mother."

Rose got out of the car. She and Esther Feinstein looked at each other, somehow recognizing a kindred spirit, two victims of life's most terrible loss. Suddenly Rose did not want to solve crimes any more. She didn't want to accumulate clues, or find pieces to puzzles. She wanted to do anything she could to comfort this woman.

"I'm Rose Bevelacqua," she said, extending her hand. "Let's go upstairs."

They passed Asad's door and paused in front of Carl's. Ira Feinstein used a key to unlock it and they went inside.

The apartment wasn't the typical bachelor pad. There were no posters of swimsuit models or rock bands; the only wall ornamentation was calendar. The room seemed to be divided into two functional halves—the music side, which was full of light from a tall narrow window, and the computer side, which was enshrouded in shadow by the sheet of plywood covering the window where Carl fell. On the music side, a cello rested on a metal support beside a music stand and a wooden chair. On the computer side, a laptop lay on a narrow desk tucked into a niche beside a closet. In addition to the laptop, the little desk also held a table lamp and a twelve-compartment plastic chest of the kind often used for nails and screws, but which now held flash drives. Carl and Greg seemed to have shared a sofa and coffee table that bridged their very different lives.

"How did you know Carl?" Ira asked suddenly.

"Not well at all," Murray said. "We lived in the same apartment building as his friend Betsy."

"I haven't met Betsy," Esther said. Her voice was huskier than Rose had expected. "I've heard about her—Carl had a hard time making friends, but Betsy was special to him. We were always grateful when we heard about someone he liked, and who seemed to like him back."

"He didn't get along well with Greg?" Rose asked.

"They got along well enough because Greg was never here," Esther answered. "Our impression was that Greg just wanted a place to sleep and park his cello. And that's not the kind of roommate Carl needed. Left on his own, Carl tended to get in trouble. He thought money fixed everything, so the whole point of life was just to get as much money as possible, any way you could. I don't know why I'm telling you this."

"It's all right," Rose said. "You don't understand how this could have happened, so you're trying to find some way to explain."

"Yes," Esther said, relieved. "That's it exactly."

"Carl wasn't a bad boy," Ira put in. "He was smart—he was too smart. He could have used his brains for all kinds of positive ends. But I found out last week he wasn't doing that."

"You found out about the hacking," Murray said.

"You knew?" Esther cried. "Did everyone know?"

"No, I'm pretty sure they didn't," Rose assured her. "I don't think the police knew—or at least, I don't think they knew it was Carl."

"Carl just had too much money, you see." Esther turned her huge brown eyes on Rose. "He always seemed to have too much money. Everything he had was password protected—his computer, his flash drives, his phone—so we couldn't check any of his records. But when he came to Florida to see us on winter break, Ira overheard him talking on the phone. It was clear they were talking about hacking into the university computer system. We should have confronted him then, but we didn't—we agonized over it for weeks. If we turned him in, there was always the chance he'd go to jail—if he went ahead with his plan, he'd be committing a felony, and we would have known it all along. Carl went back to school and everything seemed fine—but of course, it wasn't, because we knew what he planned to do. Finally Ira flew north to talk to Carl, to tell him to quit the hacking—he was risking everything, and for what? It wasn't a game."

Rose noticed Ira's eyes traveling around the room as his wife talked, and his gaze finally settled on one of the two bookcases flanking the tall windows. She watched his eyes move as they read each shelf and then moved to the other bookcase and read that one as well, a kind of desperation in his face.

"He's looking for the Haggadah," Esther said. "Ira, it's gone."

Murray pointed to an empty spot in the right-hand bookcase. "I saw it there in Betsy's photo of Carl. But it's not there now."

"It was my great-grandfather's—a beautiful volume, tooled in leather," Ira said. "He sent his teenage son, my grandfather, out of Germany to Switzerland with this book hidden amongst his things. My great-grandfather died at Auschwitz. My grandfather brought the book with him when he emigrated to America. It has been in our family ever since; the oldest son gives it to the oldest son at his bar mitzvah."

"And Carl was your oldest son?" Rose asked Esther.

"Carl was our only son," Esther said.

"And you think it's here?" Rose went to the bookcase and began running her fingers over the books, most of which were paperbacks and perfectly ordinary.

"No, I don't," Ira said. "The afternoon of the day Carl died, I drove up to Binghamton and yelled at him. I told him I wanted the Haggadah back because he had betrayed his great-grandfather. And he took the book, opened the window, and threw it out. I cursed him—I cursed my only son—and I ran downstairs to look for the book. It wasn't there. I was so angry I didn't want to see him—I just got in my car and drove back home."

"You didn't go back upstairs?" Rose asked. "He didn't tell you he had nothing more to say to you?"

Esther and Ira exchanged bewildered glances.

"No, he never said that," Ira said. "He said a lot of things, but he never said that."

"Aha!" said Murray suddenly. "Call the Binghamton police department, and ask for Detective Bevelacqua. Ask him whether by any chance they found a leather-bound book in Hebrew amongst the evidence they gathered on the day Carl—died."

"That's right!" Rose said. "If it had fallen out the window, the crime scene people would have picked it up, and they're probably holding it as evidence. I'm sure they'll give it back to you when the case is closed."

Rose and Murray spent an hour helping the Feinsteins pack up Carl's few belongings and put them in the Honda. Before Ira and Esther left, Murray picked up bagels, cream cheese and coffee from the Dunkin' Donuts down the street, and they all ate lunch on the coffee table in Carl's apartment. Rose and Esther exchanged phone numbers and promised to keep in touch.

Back in Murray's car, Rose was quiet. They had nearly arrived at their apartment building when suddenly she said, "I still don't get the part about the phone."

"The phone?" Murray asked.

"Betsy's phone. She wasn't on Facebook, or Instagram, or Twitter. But she stared at the phone all the time. She had to have been looking at pictures she'd taken in the past. At first she left the phone lying around on the counter; then she got paranoid that someone was going to steal it, so she never set it down. Remember she said to us that if you let other people use your phone, sometimes things get erased and they're gone forever?"

"So somebody—probably at the Cakery—got ahold of her phone and deleted a picture from it—maybe more than one. But they didn't get the right one, so they had to keep trying. And the more they tried, the more desperately Betsy hung onto her phone. She had it with her at the bus station but it wasn't found among her effects when her body was discovered. The only thing I can conclude is that she hid it in the motel room and it's still there."

"But if she hid it at the motel, wouldn't the staff have found it? Or the forensics guys?"

"Maybe they weren't very good forensics guys." Rose looked at her watch. "It's still only noon. Would you like to go to Newburgh?"

"Newburgh?" Murray asked. "Now?"

"Right now," Rose said decisively.

Chapter Twenty-Two
Thursday, February 12
1:00 p.m.

Afterwards, Rose thought she and Murray should have used their driving time on the way to Newburgh analyzing the case. But truthfully, the intricacies of two murders were beginning to overwhelm her. She and Murray had been too many places, talked to too many people, and their conversation with the Feinsteins had reopened the unhealed wound of Anthony's death. Murray seemed to sense that, and suggested breaking open a brand-new double CD of the greatest hits of the fifties.

All the way down route 17 and across 84, they sang along with Pat Boone, Patsy Cline, Little Richard and Bobby Vinton. In between songs they particularly loved, they would recall memories of growing up in New York's Southern Tier. As a girl, Rose hadn't been particularly aware there were Jewish people living around her—everyone she knew was Catholic—and while Murray said he'd been all too aware of his region's Christian culture, all his boyhood friends and relatives had been Jewish. So Rose was fascinated to discover how that American pop music had formed the soundtrack for both their lives. Murray's first kiss took place at the Airport Drive-in while "Puppy Love" played on the radio. Rose lifted her cousin Marie's record of "Unchained Melody" and deliberately failed to return it (an act she never admitted to in confession lest Father D'Amato might tell her to give it back). Both she and Murray agonized over their first dance to Jimmie Rodger's "Honeycomb"—Rose's with Tommy Roma at the CYO, and Murray's with Lydia Buchberg at the JCC. All of Rose and

Murray's four sets of grandparents hated rock and roll, and bought them musical instruments they felt would encourage them to learn traditional music; Rose hated the accordion and would not play it, while Murray developed a tremendous affection for the clarinet, an instrument he still played to this day.

But it was plain that as children, and even as teenagers, they were very much the same. Rose wondered why Catholics of her parents' generation, and even of her own, saw Jews as belonging to an entirely different species.

When they got off the highway at Newburgh, they pulled into a gas station and Rose sent Murray inside to ask for directions. When he returned to the car, he did a little happy dance before getting in.

"Apparently Betsy's been the talk of Newburgh," he said. "The motel's right down this road and then left. It's pretty close to the bus station, which shouldn't come as much of a surprise."

They drove to the motel and parked opposite the office.

"Now," Rose said, laying her hand on Murray's knee, "let's get our story straight before we go in. We tend to approach people with no pretext whatsoever, and then we're covering each other's butts as we go along."

"But that's half the fun!" Murray protested.

"Not for me, it's not," Rose said. "I can't think on my feet like you can. My feet are old."

"My feet are older."

"Whatever. Now think. Why do we want to spend the night in the same room where Betsy was killed?"

"We're spending the night?" Murray asked. "Together? Who's paying for this?"

"You are, and no, we're not really spending the night in a motel room together. But if we just say we want to search

159

Betsy's room, the innkeeper won't let us in—or he won't leave us alone. Now, why do we want that particular room?"

"We stayed there on our honeymoon sixty years ago?" Murray suggested.

Rose rolled her eyes. "Murray. Look around you. This motel isn't sixty years old, and I would have been fourteen when we married. Try again."

"We're ghostbusters."

"Not bad," Rose admitted grudgingly.

The innkeeper turned out to be a grizzled Indian man who had no difficulty fathoming why two retired Americans would want to hunt ghosts. In fact, he found it fascinating. "You probably have Geiger counters and tape recorders and heat sensors—stuff like that?" he asked.

"In the trunk," Murray said smoothly. "We generally don't take them out unless we perceive the spirit to be particularly strong. And we can generally tell within the first half-hour."

"Oh, the spirit is strong," the man assured him. "That girl didn't want to die."

"What makes you think so?" Rose asked.

"She came on a Wednesday. Late afternoon. She had no luggage, no rucksack, nothing but her purse, and she was scared. She asked me for a room that was secure. I told her all my rooms are secure, but she wanted second floor, near surveillance camera."

"So there's a video of the attack?"

"The police asked that too," said the innkeeper. "No videotape in the camera. Do you know how hard it is to find videotape these days? And the expense. I'd be out of business in a month. So you want to see the room? You need to pay first. That's what I told the girl who died, and she paid cash for the first two nights. Never did get paid for the third night, of course, because she wasn't alive to pay me."

With a grouchy side glance at Rose, Murray proffered his credit card and signed his name.

"When you get done here, there are other places to see nearby," the innkeeper suggested. "At a pub in Poughkeepsie, two cousins were picked up by a serial killer. And in Stanfordville, an entire family was found murdered on a farm. But I'm sure you'll be happy in Room 223. Very active spirit."

Key in hand, Rose and Murray took the elevator to the second floor and went down a long corridor before at last arriving at Room 223. Once inside, it took Rose's eyes a minute to adjust to the darkness. It was clear that any trace of Betsy's stay at the motel had been carefully erased. Rose and Murray peered under the bed and between the mattress and box spring, and carefully felt inside each drawer and cabinet and across the full length and depth of the closet shelf. Nothing. Probably because it had so recently been a crime scene, Room 223 was cleaner than most motel rooms were likely to be.

"So that's that," Murray said, sinking down onto the bed. "Bupkus."

"Don't give up yet," Rose said. Taking a small slip of paper from her purse, she used the hotel phone to make a long-distance call to a Binghamton number.

She waited. And waited. Nothing happened.

"I must have done that wrong," she said. She repeated what she'd just done, with the same results. Nothing.

"You know," said Murray, "the definition of insanity is doing the same thing over and over and expecting different results."

"Shut up," Rose said. This time she dialed a different long-distance number.

Parker answered the phone a bit tentatively. "Hello?"

"Parks, it's Nonni."

"Nonni, where in the world are you? This isn't your number. And what area code is this?"

"Never mind. I'm on a day trip with Murray but we'll be home later tonight. I have a question for you, though. If you leave a cell phone alone for a week, is it dead? I mean, does it need to be charged before it would answer calls?"

"Yes, it definitely would need to be charged," Parker said. "Otherwise it wouldn't even ring."

"Well, that explains that," Rose said. "How about if you turned it off for a whole week and then turned it back on? Would it ring then?"

"That's iffy. I would think so, but I'm not sure. But you know, you can buy a universal charger at the drug store, if that's your problem."

"I have to find the phone first," Rose said, and hung up.

With a determined sigh, she got down on her hands and knees and crawled over to the edge of the wall-to-wall carpeting, moving her fingers along the edge of the wall. "It's got to be here. Betsy couldn't leave it alone—she had to look at her photos—but the police said they didn't find it. So she had to have hidden it really, really well. Are you going to help me look for it or not?"

Disgruntled, Murray got down on his hands and knees on the opposite side of the room and began pressing the edge of the carpet. "Why do you think it's under the rug?"

"Because the carpeting is loose over there by the bathroom," Rose said, "and we've looked everyplace else.".

A half-hour later, they had covered every square inch of the green shag carpet. There was no phone.

"Look under the drawers in the dresser," Rose commanded.

"Are you kidding?" Murray said. "I woke up at six o'clock this morning, I've driven for three hours straight, and I've crawled around on my hands and knees for thirty minutes. It's time for my nap."

He slipped off his shoes and lay down on the bed.

"Well, I'm not joining you, if that's what you're thinking," Rose said stiffly.

"I thought no such thing," Murray said. "I'm simply telling you, I'll be fresh as a daisy in an hour and a half, but I'll never make it home without a nap."

"Well, I'm looking under all the dresser drawers," Rose said. "And inside the vanity. And inside the toilet tank."

"Knock yourself out," Murray told her. "Wake me up when you're done."

After five or ten minutes, Murray started to snore softly. He flopped onto his back and his snores got louder. Rose checked every spot she'd mentioned and thought of a few more, but there was absolutely no phone in the room. She sat on the edge of the bed, frustrated.

Suddenly she jumped to her feet, grabbed the room key from the desk, and dashed down to the motel office. The Indian man was watching a talk show.

"By any chance," Rose asked, "did you find a Smartphone in the hotel room where we're staying?"

The Indian looked over at her, clearly weighing his response. "Those Smartphones. Very expensive. Might cost five hundred dollars. Six, even. Or seven."

"I've heard that," Rose said, barely able to contain her excitement. "But used ones—cheap ones with sticker residue on them, for instance—they wouldn't go for so much."

"No," the Indian man agreed. "They might only go for two, three hundred."

"Or one," Rose said. "Because the girl who owned that phone only owed you for one night's stay. She paid you a hundred dollars a night for the first two nights, and then before she paid you for the third night, she died. So if we pay you for the phone, you'll give it to me, right? Because that's what you were going to do, wasn't it—sell the phone to recoup the money you didn't get from her."

"You drive a hard bargain," the man said. "But one hundred dollars would do."

"I'll be right back," Rose told him. She scurried back to her motel room, where Murray was sleeping the sleep of the just.

"Wake up," she demanded. "You've got to go down to the office and pay that Indian man a hundred dollars. If you don't have a hundred dollars, put it on your credit card."

"I—what?" Murray mumbled, and then his eyes snapped open as Rose's words hit home. "I just paid him a hundred dollars. Why do I have to pay him again?"

"Because he's got Betsy's phone, and he's not going to give it to us unless we pay him for it."

Murray sat up stiffly. "How long did I sleep?"

"About a half an hour. But if you go down and pay that man to get Betsy's phone, you can sleep until doomsday as far as I'm concerned."

"You know why I put up with you?" Murray grumbled. "You remind me of my Aunt Minna. She was my favorite aunt. She was like a bulldog, that one. And so are you."

"Fine, wonderful," Rose said. "Take your credit card down to the office and get the phone."

Five minutes later, Murray returned and tossed the familiar sticker-covered phone at Rose. "You were right," he said. "It was turned off and under the rug. The owner spotted the bump in the carpeting while he was calling the police."

Rose held the black-screened phone in her hand almost reverently. Murray went back to sleep for an hour as Rose pressed various buttons on the side of the phone and then touched the camera icon on the home page. She took a picture of Murray asleep on the bed; the phone saved her photo to the gallery and displayed all the other images saved there as well. Amazed, Rose identified a picture of Greg playing the cello in some outdoor venue; a picture of Greg eating a bagel at the Cakery; a picture of Carl and Greg laughing at some long-forgotten joke; the selfie Betsy took with Greg at Carnegie Hall. Picture after picture, dozens of them, almost all Greg. Rose could see how someone as obsessed as Betsy could spend hours looking at this tiny electronic scrapbook—as indeed it seemed Betsy had.

She continued to hold the phone all the way back to Binghamton; it felt warm in her hand, almost as if Betsy had momentarily come back to life.

Somewhere near Roscoe, she had a terrible thought.

"Murray? Smartphones have GPSes built into them, don't they?"

"I guess so. Why?"

"Well, couldn't somebody track our location using Betsy's phone?"

"Maybe. Not sure. I really don't know anything about Smartphones." Murray drove a little further into the darkness. "I did see a mystery show on television where a man was locked in a freezer with his cell phone but couldn't call for help because the freezer wall blocked the signal. So he froze to death. I don't know if that really happens, though."

"What does that have to do with the price of beans?" Rose asked. "We're not in a freezer, we're in a Cadillac. I just don't want the bad guys, whoever the bad guys are, to be able to track us all the way home."

"Well, if they can, they can. I really don't think there's anything you can do about it."

Rose didn't think so either. She only knew that the answer to the mystery had to be on that phone, and she strongly suspected that anyone possessing that phone was in very grave danger indeed. She resolved that when she got home, she'd put the phone in the freezer—just in case.

Chapter Twenty-Three
Friday, February 13
10:00 a.m.

Normally, Rose's unwavering circadian rhythms always woke her up at 7:00, and her body began to anticipate sleep around ten. Her late night trip home from Newburgh, though, had thrown her off completely. She and Murray didn't get back to the apartment until after eleven, and by then her mind was racing, turning over every possibility, analyzing everything that could be a potential clue. It was nearly three before she finally slept.

So it should have come as no surprise when an insistent rapping at the door awoke her from a dead sleep at ten a.m. She swung her feet over the edge of the bed, threw on her terrycloth robe, and allowed herself a necessary trip to the bathroom before answering the door.

Through the peephole, she saw a very pretty young woman with Betsy's brown eyes and Betsy's heart-shaped face. But this young woman had a lovely figure unlike Betsy's lumpy snowman shape, shimmering, beautifully-cut hair, and flattering clothes. Her smile revealed teeth much straighter and whiter than Betsy's had been. She held four or five nested cardboard boxes.

Rose opened the door.

"Mrs. Bevelacqua? I'm Sara Mangero. You asked me to call me when I got into town, but I figured that since I knew Betsy's address, I'd be able to find my way. I'm sorry I woke you though."

"Sara, I should be the one apologizing. I overslept. Please come in—I'll make you a cup of tea."

"That's okay," Sara said. "I got takeout on the way. If you wouldn't mind letting me into my sister's apartment, though, I'll get started sorting through her things."

This was a conundrum. Rose wanted to trust Sara—after all, she was Betsy's sister—but she wanted to observe the items Sara chose to keep and those she wanted to discard. She also wanted to understand Sara a little better before she completely trusted her. Sara was the last person in Betsy's immediate circle that Rose really didn't know.

"Hang on just a minute," Rose said. "I'll be right back."

Leaving Sara in the open doorway, she hurried back into her apartment, whipped off her nightclothes, and pulled on a pair of stretch pants, a bra, a tee shirt, and a lightweight zipped hoodie. She popped a breath mint into her mouth, grabbed her previously-bent paper clips from the desk drawer, and rejoined Sara at the door.

"All set," she said cheerfully. "Now for a bit of lock-picking."

"You don't have a key to Betsy's apartment?" Sara asked.

Rose shook her head. "At Christmastime, Betsy went to New York City and gave me the key so I could feed the cat. But when she came home, she took her key back."

"That must have been when she went to see Greg perform at Carnegie Hall," Sara said.

"You knew about that?" Rose asked, twisting her paper clips in the lock. "I'm sorry—I just assumed you and Greg weren't still close."

"We parted pretty amiably. We just chose colleges so far apart that a long-distance relationship wasn't practical. I think in the back of our minds, we always thought that we might get back together."

"Do you think you will?"

Sara shrugged. "I'd say probably not, but it's really too early to tell. We're both starting to get our names out there and establish our careers."

"But you keep in touch?"

"We definitely keep in touch," Sara said with a smile. "I would have gone to the concert in New York City this Christmas, but then Greg told me he thought Betsy was coming, and she and I haven't been getting along well lately. So I figured there would be other concerts."

Rose popped the door open, thinking that she would never understand young people and their complicated relationships.

They both went into Betsy's apartment, just as tidy and untouched as it had seemed the week before.

"Like here's an example," Sara commented, picking up an 8x10 photo on the end table. The photo was an enlargement of the same selfie of Greg and Betsy that Rose had glimpsed on Betsy's phone. Greg was wearing a tuxedo; Betsy was wearing a puffy winter coat; and they seemed to be in some sort of recital space with some men chatting in the background. "I'm sure that's from the Carnegie Hall concert. I gave Betsy a cell phone for her birthday last year, and she got obsessed with taking pictures. Some were selfies with another person; some were just shots of random people—I mean, they probably weren't random to Betsy, I'm sure, but there was no real significance to them."

"They had significance to her," Rose said. "She loved to look at those photos."

"I know, but not everybody likes having their photo taken by some strange woman. Betsy totally didn't get that." Sara stared thoughtfully at the picture for a while, then put it back on the table. "I'm not sure I want to keep that one. It's kind of sad."

The two people in the foreground of the picture were smiling happily—Greg flushed in the afterglow of a great concert, and Betsy basking in the aura of someone she loved. "Why is it sad?" Rose asked.

"It's just a story," Sara said. "She made up this whole story about how I was keeping her apart from Greg, and if I stayed out of the picture Greg would realize it was Betsy he'd loved all along. You lived across the hall from her. Didn't she make up stories for you?"

And Rose remembered with a shock that Betsy had, indeed, made up stories for her. How she'd saved a man's life on the bus when he choked on a bagel—a story. According to her favorite bus driver, the man had really just swallowed hard, and Betsy actually caused a panic on the bus by screaming until the driver called 911. Then there was the story of how she'd rescued her cat Daniel from a Chinese chef determined to turn him into chow mein. Rose was sure Betsy had simply found the cat on the street near a Chinese restaurant. How her sister had stolen all her friends— undoubtedly a story; Sara seemed quite capable of making friends on her own, while Betsy did not.

Was Carl being pushed out of the window also a story? Did Betsy also make up the story of the serial killer with the silver eyes?

Vincent had talked to Betsy for five minutes and told his mother Betsy wasn't a credible witness. Was she a credible witness about anything?

Over the next hour, Sara and Rose sorted and packed until there were four neat boxes of momentos, one cat carrier complete with cat, and many more things stuffed into plastic bags to donate to the Salvation Army. And they talked. Sara, the elder sister by two years, said Betsy had always wanted to do everything Sara did. But whereas Sara sailed through school and social settings with effortless ease, Betsy found everything more difficult. She compensated by creating an elaborate fantasy life in which she was the princess, she was the heroine, and often, she was the victim. When her fantasy life collided with reality, trouble ensued.

"When Betsy decided to move to Binghamton to follow Greg, I was worried," Sara said. "I talked to her counselor, and her counselor talked to Betsy, but in the end there was nothing either of us could do. It was really hard to talk Betsy out of her fantasies, and this one was particularly tenacious. She had no history of violence, either toward herself or anyone else, so we couldn't stop her from going. Her counselor just made sure she had a decent job and a safe place to live, and off she went. Greg, actually, was the one who kept me informed on how she was doing."

"But she told me Greg took out a restraining order on her," Rose said.

"Well, he didn't quite. He was, you know, seeing somebody, and Betsy was following them around, taking pictures of them together. So Greg contacted the police and told them she was harassing him. He said he didn't want to press charges, but could they please talk to Betsy and tell her that if she kept coming around and taking pictures, he would."

"Who was he seeing?" Rose asked.

"You'll have to ask him," Sara said. "I wouldn't know her anyway."

"Do you know why Betsy went to Newburgh?"

Sara smiled sadly. "I think I do, yes. When we were kids, my grandparents had a summer home close to Newburgh. Betsy and I would go there for the weekend, and on Sunday night my parents would drive out from Litchfield to pick us up. I suspect Betsy may have thought that if she went to

Grandma's, she would be safe. Of course, Grandma isn't there any more."

By now they'd sealed the boxes and carried them into the hallway that separated Betsy's apartment from Rose's. Sara turned to Rose and gave her a quick spontaneous hug.

"I'd like to get back on the road," she said. "But I want to thank you for letting me into Betsy's apartment, and being so understanding. The police are keeping all of Betsy's effects until the investigation is closed, and that would of course include her purse, her phone, and her keys—which would have made it kind of hard for me to get in without your help."

Rose opened her mouth to correct her, and then shut it again. She knew Betsy's phone, at least, was in her freezer, not at the police station.

"Don't you want to come over to my place for a bite of lunch before you leave?" she asked. "I've got some nice boiled ham and provolone cheese—we could have grilled sandwiches. And I make a delicious strawberry lemonade."

"How could I turn that down?" Sara asked. "Let me set these boxes in the car and I'll be right back up."

Rose assembled the sandwiches and set them in a cast iron skillet to toast while she poured bottled lemonade into a glass pitcher. She planned to muddle frozen strawberries into the bottom of the pitcher, but in the process of digging the strawberries out from behind the pot roast, the frozen peas, and the ice cream, she knocked the strawberries, a package of peas, and an ice pack onto the floor. Hearing Sara's footsteps on the stairs, she snatched up the strawberries and was just emptying them into the pitcher when Sara reappeared.

"It looks like your sandwiches are done," she said. "And are these tumblers in the dish drainer okay to use? That lemonade looks amazing."

"It's an easy cheat," Rose told her, still bent over the pitcher and smashing strawberries. "The lemonade wasn't cold, so I'm using the frozen strawberries in place of ice."

"Too late," Sara said.

Turning around, Rose saw Sara holding two tumblers already filled with ice cubes.

"I can put them back in the freezer...." Sara offered.

"No need," Rose said. "The lemonade will just be really cold, that's all." They chose plates from the dish drainer and sat down at the kitchen table with their lunch.

"These sandwiches are fabulous," Sara said. "Did you put just the tiniest touch of mustard on the bread? And the lemonade is perfect—tart and sweet, in just the right balance. I know this isn't cordon bleu, but I'll bet you're a terrific cook."

"I like to think so," Rose said modestly. Sara seemed so charming and normal; it was hard to imagine she was Betsy's sister.

After lunch, Sara gathered up the cat from his comfy chair by the living room window and put him in the carrier she'd brought to take him home. "I'll be back in a week or two to help dispose of the furniture," she said. "I'm sure the landlord would like the stuff out of here by the first of the month."

"I'm sure he would, yes." This was the first time that Rose realized that soon she'd have a new neighbor—one who might not be as flaky as Betsy, but wouldn't come with Betsy's odd and endearing little quirks. Again, inexplicably, she thought of Anthony, and her eyes teared.

"Don't start," Sara said. "Just say goodbye, and I'll see you soon."

And with another hug, she was gone.

Rose returned to the kitchen. About halfway through the process of clearing the dishes, she remembered Betsy's phone, and looked in the freezer for it. It wasn't there.

She rifled through the frosty frozen food, unable to believe it. Sara had taken the phone! Rose wouldn't have thought anything about it if Sara had mentioned finding it—after all, with all those Hello Kitty stickers, it had clearly belonged to her sister. But just to take it? Just like that? She must have spotted it when she was getting the ice cubes, and then sat through lunch, all charming and delightful and "What wonderful lemonade you make," without mentioning anything about it.

Rose was baffled. She'd liked Sara so much—but could Sara actually be a suspect?

Chapter Twenty-Four
Friday, February 13
1:00 p.m.

Rose sat down with her steno pad and recorded the conversation with Sara as nearly as she could recall it. Then she added the detail of the missing phone. She noticed that her steno pad was nearly filled, with only four blank pages remaining. The cover of the pad said there were eighty sheets. This meant she'd filled seventy-six pages, front and back, with writing, and she felt no closer to figuring out who killed Carl and Betsy than she had when she began page one. And now she had added Sara.

She called Murray to fill him in on her morning visitor. He answered immediately, which meant he was either standing by the phone or sitting beside it.

"You have to help me," Rose said.

"What's wrong?" Murray asked anxiously. "Are you hurt?"

"Hurt?" she asked. "Why would I be hurt? Betsy's sister Sara was here. She took the cat, and some of Betsy's things—"

"You're sure you're okay?"

"Of course I'm okay. But while she was here—"

Murray interrupted. "My son David is waiting for me. He's going to drive me to the doctor for an eye test. They might put those drops in my eyes, which is why I need a ride."

"Can you call me when you get back? I really need to talk to you."

"No," Murray said. "I'm going to David's afterwards for Shabbat dinner."

"You're staying down there until tomorrow?"

"No, I'll walk home after dinner. It's not far."

"So call me when you get home."

"I can't," Murray reminded her. "It's Shabbat. I don't—do that thing—on Shabbat."

"What thing?"

His voice dropped to a whisper. "Solve crimes."

"Right," Rose said. "So call me from David's. After your eye test."

There was a long pause. "I don't think that's a good idea. I'll pick you up for the concert tomorrow night."

"Tomorrow *night*?" Rose shrieked.

"Did you forget we're going to Greg's concert tomorrow night? Are you sure you're okay?"

"I'm perfectly fine," Rose said between gritted teeth, and hung up.

Somebody had to help her figure this out, because she was way over her head. She called the next most likely person.

"North Tower Five," Diane said.

"Can you and Parker come over for dinner tonight?"

"Mom, wouldn't you have been embarrassed if somebody else answered?"

"I don't care who answers, as long as they come over and help me unravel this mystery," Rose said.

Diane laughed. "I'd love to, Mom, honestly. But I can't, and neither can Parker. She's got a guard show tonight."

"I thought guard shows were on Saturday."

"Most of them are. This one isn't."

"Can't she skip it? She's a really essential part of my investigative team."

"Flattery will get you nowhere," Diane said. "But you've seen a guard show. You know they need every single member there for the show to go off well. You'll have to wait until tomorrow."

"I'm sick of waiting until tomorrow," Rose said, and hung up.

Flopping back in her chair, she tapped the steno pad on her knee as she thought. When she was in high school, her history teacher had taught her to write a research paper by writing each fact on a single index card. "Abraham Lincoln's mother was Nancy Hanks." "Abraham Lincoln's vice-president was Andrew Johnson." And then, when she got ready to write her report, she could reassemble all the cards from various sources and come out with a coherent narrative. Would this work for solving a mystery? It couldn't hurt....

And while she didn't have any index cards, she just so happened to have something very similar—recipe cards, which she bought by the gross. She unwrapped a fresh package and began to write.

Four hours later, she was into her third pack when the flash of inspiration finally came. She jumped to her feet, grabbed the two bent paper clips from her desk drawer, and broke into Betsy's apartment for the third time. The photo that Sara hadn't wanted—the one that just told a story—still sat on the end table in the living room. Greg's face was pressed close to Betsy's, their hair intermingled, their cheekbones touching. And in the background, over Greg's shoulder, there were two men, talking.

Rose didn't recognize either one of them. But she thought she knew who they were.

Scurrying back into her apartment, she picked up her coat and purse and ran down the stairs, realizing that when the adrenaline wasn't pumping, her legs would demand retribution. At the corner, she stamped her feet impatiently until the eastbound bus came, and she rode downtown as far as she could. Then she got off the bus and strode the remaining four blocks to the public library.

The woman at the reference desk looked up brightly. "Can I help you?"

"Yes," Rose said. "My granddaughter, who has a Smartphone, looked up an article about something that happened at a college in Delaware a couple of years ago. Do you have computers that could do the same thing?"

"Certainly," the woman said. "You could use a public access computer, or I could look it up for you right here."

"Please do that," Rose said.

She explained about the hacking scandal at Delaware Tech, and the librarian found it on the computer without any difficulty.

"Now, can you find an article about a similar scheme that was organized by a professor on Long Island?"

The librarian found this as well. "The professor was named Simon McKendrick. But he's not a professor there anymore; the university suspended him without pay."

"When did they do that?" Rose asked.

"January 10th. About a month ago."

"Can you find a picture of him?"

The university's website, it turned out, no longer included him in their faculty list. But there was a photo of his arrest from the original news article when the scandal broke. He looked scruffier and much less professional than he did in the background of Betsy's selfie. But it was clearly the same man.

"Is there any way you could print that out?" Rose asked.

"It costs fifteen cents per page. You'll probably get the whole article with it."

"Not a problem," Rose said. "I'm good for it."

Holding the photo in her hand, Rose knew her next question would give her the other part of the puzzle, so she took a deep breath before she phrased it. The librarian's fingers flew over the keys and like magic, a second image appeared on the screen.

"Print that one too," Rose said. "Please."

When she received the second photo, she stared at it for a long time. Then she rolled it up with the first and put both sheets in her purse.

It was starting to get dark as she left the library, and the streetlights had come on. Rose's whole body hurt from a day of unaccustomed exertion. But the most painful thing was having a puzzle close enough to completion that she could see the outlines, recognize the people, and see what happened—and she had no one to share it with, no one to tell. Was it time to call Vincent? It just might be. She got on the #35 bus and headed west.

When she got back to the apartment, she sat down in her accustomed spot on the couch, picked up the telephone receiver, and dialed Vincent's number.

The voice that answered wasn't Vincent. "Detective unit, this is Thrasher."

Rose struggled to keep her voice even. "Ben, this is Rose Bevelacqua, Vincent's mom. Is he there, please?"

"Sorry, Mrs. B. He's out for the evening. Is there some way I could help you?"

"No, thanks, Ben. I really just wanted to talk to Vincent."

"Actually, Mrs. B, he's on a date. If it's an emergency, you can talk to me. Otherwise, you could try Vince's cell."

"Thank you, Ben," she said sweetly. "Don't worry about it."

She pressed the button on the phone's cradle to end the call. Then she took a deep breath. "So sorry to disrupt your date, lover boy," she said aloud, and called Vincent's cell number.

The phone rang once. Twice. Three times. Four. And then it went to voicemail.

"You've reached Vince Bevelacqua. I'm sorry I can't take your call right now, but leave a message at the beep and I'll return your call as soon as I can."

"So much for the wonders of cell phones," Rose said, banging the handset into its cradle so hard that the ringer jangled.

Suddenly the efforts of the two past weeks caught up with her, and she realized she was exhausted. She removed the photographs from her purse, folded them in half, and put them in her steno pad. Then she wrapped all the recipe cards in rubber bands and fastened them to the pad as well. Scanning her apartment for a hiding spot, her eyes lit on her dress form. She expanded the form to its most generous proportions, slipped the steno pad into the chest cavity, and shrunk the dress form to a svelte size eight.

And then she stripped off her clothes, put on her nightgown, climbed into bed, and turned off the light.

*   *   *

Rose was asleep in no time. But it seemed she had only been asleep a few minutes before her eyes snapped open again. She had lived in this apartment for several years, and by now she knew every sound made by plumbing or wind or noisy neighbors. This was none of those. There was someone in her room. She reached for the phone to dial 911, only to have a latex-gloved hand cover hers and replace the phone in its cradle.

"Don't scream," a low-pitched male voice commanded quietly. "Just give me the cell phone you took from the motel."

"I don't have it," Rose said.

"Don't lie to me," the man said. He grabbed her arm and pulled her to her feet. Her tired knees buckled beneath her, but he yanked her upwards again. "Go get the phone."

The moonlight fell on his face as he turned toward the window.

"I know who you are, you know," she said. "Betsy had a picture of you at Carnegie Hall this Christmas. And that's why you want the phone. Either you weren't supposed to be there in the first place, or you weren't supposed to be talking to the guy you were talking to."

"Give me the phone," he repeated.

"I'd love to," Rose said, "But I honestly don't know where it is. I put it in the freezer, but I think Betsy's sister took it out."

Still dragging Rose behind him, the man went into the kitchen and opened the freezer door. A dim light came on, and Rose saw the desperation in his face as he rummaged through her frozen food. He leaned further into the unit, stretching all the way to the back, and Rose felt his grip on her arm loosen slightly. She jerked herself free and slammed the freezer door shut on his head. The intruder slumped to the ground with a moan. As Rose bolted out of the kitchen she spotted Betsy's cell phone just peeking beneath the bottom lip of the refrigerator. But the intruder was starting to move, so Rose dashed through the living room, tipping over lamps and chairs and a magazine rack, creating as much chaos as she could.

She flung open the front door, screaming, "Help me! Help me!"

For a moment, Rose had the terrible feeling that no one was going to come to her rescue. Behind her, back in the apartment, she heard the man crashing over the obstacles she'd created to slow him down. Then suddenly, Murray emerged from his apartment in his pajamas. He grabbed Rose's arm in the same spot the intruder had already bruised and whirled her through his own apartment door.

"Lock the door and call 911!" he commanded.

In the seconds before she shut the door, she glimpsed Mr. Esposito, garish in green and orange pajamas, thundering up the steps, followed by Mr. Tinkasingh and Mr. Khan. For the next twenty seconds, the hall was full of yelling in at least three different languages, and then Rose heard the sound of someone tumbling down the stairs. She shut her eyes. "Please, God," she prayed, "don't let that be Murray!"

She opened the door just a crack and almost fainted with relief to see Murray standing just outside. "He's out cold on the landing," he told her. "The men are tying him up with the belts of their bathrobes. Did you call 911? Do you know who he is?"

"Of course I know who he is," Rose said. "It's Brian Reeves. The murderer."

Chapter Twenty-Five
Saturday, February 14
9:00 a.m.

When Rose and Murray got to the station on Saturday morning, Vincent was there.

He raised a warning finger to his mother, lowered it again, and then curled it into a fist and pressed it to his mouth—a cop's way of fighting back tears. "I am so angry at you, I can't even take your statement. Why wouldn't you just tell me what you'd found out and let me handle it?"

"Because you don't listen," Rose said. "I tried to tell you Betsy was in trouble, but you said she wasn't. I tried to tell you about the phone, but all you wanted to do was yell at me about interviewing suspects. And last night I tried to call you but you were off the grip."

"Grid," said Murray and Vincent in unison.

"Grid," Rose self-corrected. "How was your date, by the way?"

"It was fine," Vincent said. Then his icicles melted. "I'm just so glad you're okay."

"Well, I'm glad too," said his mother primly.

"Especially since you made me come down here on Shabbat." Murray crabbily stroked his unshaven chin.

"Oh, don't even get me started on you, buddy," Vincent said. This time there was no tenderness in his voice. "You were supposed to stay out of this. You were supposed to keep my mother out of this."

"I don't believe I ever agreed to that," Murray told him.

"And he wasn't around half the time anyway," Rose said. "He was always Shabbatting this or Shabbatting that."

"I was around a lot!" Murray said, turning to her. "Who drove you to the university? Who drove you to Newburgh?"

"Newburgh?" Vincent asked incredulously. "You went to Newburgh?"

"Well, of course," his mother replied. "That's where we found the phone."

Vincent seemed to make a decision, and called over to his partner. "Ben, you can take their formal statements in a minute. I need to hear this."

"Figured you would," Ben said.

Vincent led his mother and Murray into a small room with a table and three chairs. "Start talking."

"Is this on the record or off?" Rose asked.

"Just talk."

Rose looked over at Murray and took a deep breath. "Okay. We started with quite a few basic assumptions, some of which weren't true. One, we assumed Carl's death was a premeditated murder rather than an accident. Brian definitely killed both Carl and Betsy, but I'm pretty sure he didn't go to Carl's apartment intending to kill him—and I don't think he went to Newburgh intending to kill Betsy, either."

"She was stabbed, Ma," Vincent pointed out. "With a really long knife. Not something everybody carries around in their car if they're not planning to use it."

"I suspect he was just planning to scare her with it. He never expected her to fight back. Do you want to hear my second erroneous assumption?"

"Go for it."

Rose wiggled her bottom to settle into the uncomfortable chair. "Two, a mysterious man came into the bakery and bought a Black Forest cake, and this man was the killer. The fact that he bought a cake, of course, was true—but he was definitely not a killer, serial or otherwise."

"So who was he?" Vincent asked.

"He was an actor, playing a part. Two different people have played the serial killer—Brian Reeves in Newburgh, and an accomplice in Binghamton where Brian would have been recognized. As to the identity of the accomplice, I'd start by questioning the Asian grad student in the Computer Science department. One day he had brown eyes and the next they were bright green, which obviously isn't natural, and it shows that he's comfortable wearing unusual contact lenses. But this isn't really about serial killers and Black Forest cake—that was my third erroneous assumption. It's really about Brian Reeves trying to get ahold of Betsy's phone."

"You lost me," Vincent said.

"Several years ago, at Delaware Tech, a guy hacked into a professor's computer to steal the answers to an important exam," Rose said. "He was in cahoots with a couple of students who sold the exam answers to people in that class. Flash forward to this fall. There was an attempt to do a much more sophisticated version of this scheme at all the state universities in New York. But there had to be one professor on each campus masterminding the whole thing, and a number of students willing and able to do the hacking. At Binghamton University, the professor masterminding the job was Brian Reeves. One of the hackers was Carl Feinstein."

"I can see Carl doing that," Murray said. "Everyone said he was obsessed with money. But why Brian Reeves? Eileen said her husband made so much money she didn't have to work."

"Yes, but Justin said Brian was always at the casino," Rose reminded him. " 'Always at the casino' frequently means 'gambling problem'."

"So how does this connect to Betsy?" Vincent wanted to know.

"Aha." Rose raised a knowing finger. "The man who developed the hacking scheme was a computer science professor at a state university on Long Island. His name is Simon McKendrick. The operation was supposed to begin during the spring semester—the semester we're currently in. McKendrick met with Brian Reeves at Carnegie Hall in New York City, after a holiday concert."

"The concert Greg Thomas played in!" Murray exclaimed.

"Exactly. And if you remember, Betsy also went to this concert, and took a very cuddly selfie with Greg. They're pressed so close together that there's a considerable amount of free space over Greg's left shoulder, and in that space—if you enlarge the photo—you can clearly see Simon McKendrick and Brian Reeves, talking. There's actually an 8x10 of this selfie in Betsy's living room, but apparently nobody came to her apartment to see it."

"So she has a picture of two computer whizzes talking," Murray said. "I don't see the problem."

"I do," Vincent said. "After McKendrick's arrest, we interrogated a number of Binghamton University guys who had flown into our radar as possible collaborators. Reeves was one of them. He swore up and down he never met McKendrick."

"But how did Brian find out he was in Betsy's selfie?" Murray asked.

"The concert was at the beginning of December," Rose said. "Betsy came home from New York City positively aglow, and with a cell phone full of photos. She showed them all to her co-workers, just as she showed them all to me. And then she sat during her lunch break and flipped through them, just fantasizing. Her favorite, of course, was the selfie she took with Greg. It's not too hard to imagine that Eileen would have looked over Betsy's shoulder and wondered what her husband was doing with Betsy at a concert in Manhattan."

"So she asked him," Vincent said.

"She must have—wouldn't you? And he probably came up with some answer logical enough to satisfy Eileen, just as he'd been explaining away his gambling problem for years. Eileen, you know, really isn't very bright, and she has a vested interest in believing her husband to be an upstanding guy who's financially secure."

"But now Brian had to destroy that picture," Murray said.

Rose nodded. "He couldn't get Eileen to delete pictures off Betsy's phone without revealing the reason. I'm betting he persuaded Samantha to do it on the grounds that Betsy had pictures of Greg and Samantha in some kind of compromising situation. Being a cougar is something best kept to oneself. Remember when Betsy first went to work at the Cakery, she showed her phone to everybody; she doesn't seem to have been overly secretive about it."

"But everybody said how paranoid she was about her phone later on," Murray pointed out. "What happened?"

"I suspect that Betsy caught Samantha fiddling with her cell phone, and realized that some pictures were missing. After that, Betsy didn't let anyone touch her phone. But unfortunately for Brian Reeves, Samantha had only deleted the photos of herself and Greg. She never got to the one photo that really mattered to Brian—the selfie at Carnegie Hall. Brian then asked Carl to steal the phone and delete the picture, but Carl's access to Betsy became limited when Samantha asked the police to keep Betsy away from Greg. Now, though, Carl knew how badly Brian needed that phone and how dangerous this could be for Betsy. He had to think of a way to save her, and this was the serial killer story."

"I don't get what the serial killer story was supposed to do," Murray said.

"I would imagine this was something Carl came up with on the spur of the moment. He was worried that Brian Reeves might do something to hurt Betsy, which turned out to be true. So if Carl couldn't get the phone, maybe he could get Betsy to disappear with it. You have to remember that that Betsy loved stories. She loved the movies; she loved TV. Carl told her a story about a serial killer who put Black Forest cake by the bodies of his victims, and he made it so real that Betsy absolutely believed it. Then he got his buddy to dress up like the imaginary serial killer and go into the shop to buy a cake. This was intended to spook Betsy so badly that she'd get on the first bus and leave town, taking her phone with her. But instead she came home and we all talked her out of it."

"If you recall," Vincent said, "I did tell you the whole thing was ridiculous."

"And it was, because it was just a story. But all Tuesday morning—while Betsy was working with Eileen—she talked about the serial killer at the university. That afternoon, Eileen went home sick, and we know that Brian doesn't work on Tuesday afternoon so we can assume he was home. Eileen must have mentioned Betsy's story to her husband, which sent Brian to Carl's apartment, armed for bear. When he got there, though, he found out Carl already had company."

"Carl's father!" Murray exclaimed.

"Exactly," Rose said. "Ira had found out about Carl's computer hacking. Carl had a valuable book that had dated from before the Holocaust, and in the middle of his argument with his father, he threw the book out the window, where it somehow didn't manage to reach the street. I figured it landed on a gable right outside the window. Vincent, I'm assuming you have it?"

Vincent nodded. "I think we do."

"Well, as soon as you can, please return it to the Feinsteins—it's an important family heirloom. Anyway, Brian overheard the argument between Carl and his father and realized that Carl was even more of a liability than he'd imagined. After Ira left, Brian went into the apartment just as Carl was hanging over the sill, trying to figure out how to retrieve the book he'd thrown out during the fight with his father. Carl must have half-turned around to ask what Brian was doing there, he and Brian began to struggle, and Carl went out the window."

Murray frowned. "But if I remember, Carl said, 'Are you back again?' Brian hadn't been there before."

"No, but at that moment Carl was half hanging out a window. He didn't realize it was Brian—he assumed it was Ira."

"So after Carl was dead," Vincent observed, "there was only one loose end. Betsy."

"I'll give Brian the benefit of the doubt and imagine that he just meant to use the knife to scare Betsy into giving him the phone, which I'm sure she'd turned off and hidden well out of sight. But that phone was the most important material thing she possessed, and she wasn't going to give up without a fight. In the struggle, she wound up getting stabbed. When he realized he'd killed her and he couldn't find the phone, he got out of there quick."

"But how did Brian find out you had the phone?" Murray asked.

"I can answer that," Vincent said. "I'll bet that sometime between Newburgh and Binghamton, my mom must have turned on the phone, which obviously still had some charge left."

"I did," Rose said. "I wanted to get a closer look at Betsy's pictures. I had the feeling, even then, that there must have been something in those pictures that Brian was willing to kill for, something that tied Carl's death to Betsy's. It did dawn on me that the killer must have used GPS to track Betsy to the motel in Newburgh, and so he could track me to Binghamton. That's why I put the phone in the freezer when I got home."

Vincent laughed affectionately. "All you needed to do was turn off the phone, you know. But by that time Reeves had tracked the phone to Madison Manor. Once inside your apartment, Reeves planned to use your cordless phone to call Betsy's. Then he'd follow the ringtone to locate the phone."

"But why would he want to use the phone in the bedroom?" Murray asked. "Why didn't he use the one in the living room?"

"I'll bet it wasn't on the base unit," Vincent answered, casting a pointed look at his mom. "Half the time, it isn't. And then when he went in the bedroom, my mom woke up and the rest is history."

"Do you think he would have killed me when he got what he wanted?" Rose asked.

Vincent nodded. "Probably, yes. You were too much of a liability."

"Well, then," Rose said. "I don't feel the least bit bad about slamming the freezer door on his head."

"But you said that after Sara came, the phone was missing," Murray said. "How did it wind up under the refrigerator?"

Rose shrugged. "I imagine it fell out while I was getting the strawberries for our lemonade. Or Sara pulled it out while she was getting the ice cubes. One of us must have accidentally kicked it under the fridge. All I know is, Sara didn't take Betsy's phone. That makes me happy because I really like her, and I didn't like believing that she was a suspect."

"There are actually a lot of innocent people in this story," Vincent said. "We've already talked to Justin Hopko, and it turns out he was constantly approached by Carl to be involved in some way in the hacking scheme. He wasn't even tempted—he wanted to get his grades the honest way."

"Greg and Samantha aren't criminals either," Murray added. "They're totally narcissistic, but not evil. Same with Eileen—she was too self-absorbed, and frankly too dumb, to notice what her husband was doing."

"But she did tell him where Betsy lived," Rose observed. "That's how he knew where to place the first slice of cake. And he probably got Betsy's number off Eileen's phone."

Vincent sat back in his chair. "Ma, I have to say I'm impressed. I can't imagine how you kept all this organized in your head."

"The steno pad!" Rose and Murray said in unison.

Vincent looked at Murray, who explained, "She wrote down all our interviews—who said what and when—in a steno pad. Don't you think that should be admitted into evidence?"

"Or at least, you might find it useful while you're preparing your case," Rose added. "It's at my apartment—I can bring it to you, or you can come pick it up when you stop by for dinner tomorrow."

"That was a hint," Murray said with a smile.

"We'll see," Vincent said. "But now, Ma, you have to promise me something."

"First I need to know what it is."

"You need to stay out of my homicide cases. It isn't safe for little old---"

"Don't you say that," Rose warned.

"For untrained amateurs to get involved with murderers. Promise me you will not do this again."

Rose crossed her fingers behind her back and smiled sweetly.

Vincent turned to Murray. "See how she is? You've got to watch her every minute."

"I wouldn't mind that," said Murray.

Epilogue
Saturday, February 14
6:00 p.m.

After she returned from the police station, Rose worked feverishly to finish her symphony dress, and by six o'clock—an hour before Murray was to pick her up—it was done. She tried it on in front of the full-length mirror in her bedroom and had to admit she'd never looked better—at least since she'd hit her seventies. The princess seams in the burgundy embroidered fabric smoothed away all her awkward bulges, and the sweetheart neckline was a perfect frame for her favorite pearls. Quickly she took the dress off, replaced it with a bathrobe, and made herself an egg-salad sandwich for dinner. Murray had promised her a celebratory dinner, but today she wanted him to be able to salvage what was left of his Shabbat.

At 6:55 she was back in her dress and putting the finishing touches on her makeup when she heard Murray's now-familiar knock. She'd hoped for a bit of a "wow" moment when she opened the door, but she was completely unprepared for what she saw.

Murray stood on her doorstep in an elegant black evening suit with a bright red silk bow tie. In his arms he held two dozen long-stemmed red roses, wrapped in crisp white paper.

"These flowers are lonely," he said. "Can you give them a home?"

"Oh, my gosh!" Rose took the flowers out of his arms and almost fainted from the intoxicating scent. "They're gorgeous. Do you do this on every date?"

As soon as the words were out of her mouth, she wanted to bite them back—wasn't it she who only a week ago had said she didn't date, and certainly would never date Murray—but she was relieved when Murray laughed.

"Only first dates that happen on Valentine's Day," he told her. "After that, my gallantry goes steadily downhill."

She transferred the roses to the only vase she had that was bit enough for all those blooms and added water. Then she let Murray help her slip into her best dress coat, and they set off downstairs toward the car.

In the glow of streetlights she could see that even the Cadillac had had a makeover; its wax job sparkled like tiny diamonds. Murray opened the passenger side door and the luxurious leather seats beckoned.

When Murray got in the driver's side, Rose said, "If you just bought the tickets to this concert to further the investigation, should we really call this a date?"

Murray had leaned forward to put the key in the ignition, but now he sat back. "Rose, we have to talk about that."

"Do we?"

"You've probably been getting mixed messages from me about whether I was interested in you romantically or not. I'm sure you're confused, because I've been confused myself. You see, my son David is very much against me dating anyone who isn't Jewish. But last night at our Shabbat dinner, I told him that I'm very fond of you and I'd like to run with this pony and see where it goes."

"Are you saying I'm a horse?" Rose asked.

"No! You're a lovely woman I enjoy very much, and if you're agreeable, I'd like to keep right on enjoying you."

"Well, that's ironic." Rose smoothed her skirt over her knees. "My daughter Diane really wants me to go out with you, and I've been resisting because I couldn't imagine dating anyone who wasn't Catholic."

Murray looked disappointed. "That *is* ironic. So that's your final decision, then?"

"No," Rose told him. "That's how I felt a week ago. Since then I've—changed. I'd like to keep enjoying you too."

"Well," Murray said. "Then I guess this is our first date. Valentine's Day. Whoever would have thought."

He leaned over a second time, put the key in the ignition, and this time the engine started to purr.

If you enjoyed *The Perfect Cake for a Lady*, you might also like its introductory novella *The Perfect Spin of a Rifle*, available on Amazon in both Kindle and paperback formats. Also, in the early fall of 2018, look for a new Rose Bevelacqua mystery, *The Perfect Saint has a Secret*. And watch for more mysteries in this series to come! Author Karen Bernardo has been very busy!

Made in the USA
Monee, IL
22 June 2026

55535801R00109